SARAH LEAN grew up in Wells, Somerset but now lives

in Dorset with her husband, son and dog. She has

worked as a page-planner for a newspaper, a stencil-

maker and a gardener, amongst various other things.

She gained a first class English degree and became a

primary school teacher before returning to complete an

MA in Creative and Critical Writing with University

of Winchester. *A Horse for Angel* is Sarah's second

novel for children.

SARAH LEAN

A horse for Angel

Illustrated by Gary Blythe

HarperCollins *Children's Books*

First published in Great Britain by
HarperCollins *Children's Books* in 2013
HarperCollins *Children's Books* is a division of HarperCollins*Publishers* Ltd,
77-85 Fulham Palace Road, Hammersmith, London, W6 8JB.

The HarperCollins website address is: www.harpercollins.co.uk

1

Copyright © Sarah Lean 2013
Illustrations © Gary Blythe

ISBN 978-0-00-745505-8

Sarah Lean asserts the moral right to be identified as the author of the work.
Gary Blythe asserts the moral right to be identified as the illustrator of
the work.

Printed and bound in England by Clays Ltd, St Ives plc

MIX
Paper from
responsible sources
FSC C007454

FSC™ is a non-profit international organisation established to promote
the responsible management of the world's forests. Products carrying the
FSC label are independently certified to assure consumers that they come
from forests that are managed to meet the social, economic and
ecological needs of present and future generations,
and other controlled sources.

Find out more about HarperCollins and the environment at
www.harpercollins.co.uk/green

For Mum

1.

Mum was late picking me up from drama club again. Which meant another twenty minutes of not wanting to be there. There was just me looking through the window as all the other children left.

Me and this boy called Jamie were extras and scenery painters, doing background colours. Which was just about all right with us, if we had to be there at all. So I thought if anyone was on my side it would be Jamie. But he wasn't. Especially not when he told Mrs Oliver that I was out the back doing dangerous things with the wiring.

Mrs Oliver blew a fuse and said I should explain myself. I looked at her and took a breath and I was about to speak, but then I didn't know what 'explaining myself' meant. You can't explain yourself. You're just you. Even though what actually happened wasn't like me at all. I'd never, ever done anything like that before.

The heat in my face made my eyes sting because I was suddenly thinking about what Mum would say.

"Well?" Mrs Oliver folded her arms.

"Well, what happened was this," I said, deciding to tell her the events like a story. "I finished doing the scenery painting, like you said, and Jamie and me had washed the brushes and we were just leaving them to dry and I found those lights… you know – the ones you were looking for? And they were in a bag with other things that needed fixing and the plug was missing and I knew how to join them to another set of lights. So I just did it, but I forgot to ask and… I didn't mean to do it."

"Nell Green, this is so unlike you," she said. What were you thinking, playing with such dangerous things?"

Which was silly because it wasn't dangerous; the lights weren't even plugged in, so nothing bad was going to happen. And maybe that made me look as if I wasn't sorry enough.

So I said, "Sorry, Mrs Oliver, I won't do it again."

Mainly I was thinking, please don't tell Mum. Which made my face flush and prickle again.

"Who knows what might have happened?" Mrs Oliver said. "What would your mother say?"

Sometimes you wish people could read your mind.

It didn't seem to matter that there was now an extra-long string of lights for the scenery. Mrs Oliver didn't expect an answer though, because she turned on her heels and clopped across the wooden floor.

So there I was with my face pushed against the window, looking as far down the road as I could to watch out for Mum's car, hoping Mrs Oliver wouldn't see Mum arrive. But she did and they discussed the incident through the car window. Now it was an *incident*, like some great big disaster.

I was belted in my seat, sandwiched between their conversation. Mrs Oliver said what an unusual skill I had, but that I should be discouraged from meddling with electrical things. Surely she meant fixing! Mum agreed instantly and gave me a look that said, *How could you?* Which was what I mostly wanted to avoid. That look.

"Maybe Nell needs more to do," Mum said. "Something more challenging to keep her occupied, Mrs Oliver. A bigger part in the play perhaps?"

One little thing was now turning into a major drama.

Keep quiet, I told myself. From Monday there's going to be two weeks of Easter holidays with Nana. Mum will be too busy with work and a conference, so there'll be no after-school clubs, no appointments, no waiting. Just me and Nana mooching about her house watching daytime TV, playing cards and computer bingo, safe and quiet. Nana doesn't drive and she won't take the bus because you never know who's sat on the seat before you or where they've been, so she can't take me to rehearsals. Hah! And Mrs Oliver was bound to forget.

Mum drove away, saying, "Do we need to have a talk?"

"No," I said. Because her betrayed face said everything.

2.

Waiting again. This time in the car while Mum rushed into the supermarket on the way home. She didn't leave the keys behind, so I couldn't open the windows or listen to the radio. I could only hear something rumbling outside and my own sighing.

Waiting makes you sigh. And sighing makes a white patch on the window so you can write

HELLO backwards.

An old lady with a trolley stopped to read my message. So I smiled. But she frowned and walked on. So I wiped the window and watched a giant thundering yellow crane instead. It turned slowly in the sky, with a big chunk of concrete swinging on a thin wire below it. I didn't blink for ages. Just watched it sway.

Mum came out of the supermarket, carrier bags in both hands, her big black handbag containing everything-anyone-could-possibly-need (and probably a hundred more things as well) weighing down her shoulder. Her phone was crushed between the strap and her ear.

I watch her face for clues and can usually work things out and guess what she's decided. She has an are-you-listening-carefully face, a don't-question-me-I-know-what-I'm-doing face and a slightly smiley making-up-for-what's-missing face the rest of the time. And I could tell two things by the way her eyes were fixed on me as she walked and talked. The two things I could tell were this: first, the phone call was about me; and second, I didn't have a choice.

"There's been a change of plan," Mum said, swinging the shopping bags into the back seat. "You're going to Aunt Liv's for the Easter holidays."

I wasn't expecting that.

"But I always stay with Nana in the holidays. Why have you changed it? Because I touched those stupid lights?"

Whatever she was about to say, she didn't.

"It has nothing to do with that."

"Yes, it is. You've changed it because of what happened earlier."

"That's not it at all. Nana's had to go up to

Leicester on the train to look after her cousin, who's had a fall. Aunty Annabel. You remember her?"

Nope. And if you fold your arms, you don't have to try to remember either.

"The one with the poodle," Mum said, and I could hear her trying hard not to make this about the incident.

I couldn't picture Aunty Annabel, just a trembling, pinkish poodle and a funny smell of ham.

"I thought you said it died."

"Yes, but you know who I mean."

"Why can't somebody else look after her? Why does it have to be Nana?"

Mum continued as if I'd said nothing.

"The decision's been made. When we get home, I want you to go up in the loft. There's a big grey suitcase up there that you're going to need."

I noticed we'd completely left out a whole

middle bit of the conversation where I could say I didn't want to go. Which is always part of Mum's master plan. Cut out the annoying middle bit and get to the point, or the next appointment. Never mind what I want.

"Start packing tonight," she said. "You can do the rest tomorrow when we get back from your maths tutor and before swimming club, then I'll drive you down to Aunt Liv's on Sunday."

I don't like drama club and I don't like the maths tutor either because her house smells of garlic. My swimming teacher says I swim like a cat, like something that doesn't want to be in the water.

My life is a list of mostly boring or pointless activities that I didn't choose, with a car drive and waiting in between. If you practise long enough, you don't have to care that everything has been taken out of your hands. That's what mums are for.

"So how was drama club? Apart from—"

"Fine," I sighed.

When we got home, we ate cold pasta salad out of supermarket cartons. Mum had her phone glued to her head again and while she was talking she waved a finger towards the loft door in the hallway ceiling at the top of the stairs.

3.

Our loft was as silent as the moon. Except for my footsteps, which sounded hollow against the boards. The yellow padding in the sloping walls blocked out the sounds of the world. It felt like a place from long ago that had stopped, with its old air and old things we keep because they don't belong at the dump or in a charity shop or anywhere else but with us.

I saw the grey suitcase. And I could have just grabbed it and gone straight back downstairs. Instead, I pushed my shoulders back and turned my chin up. I was going to make a stand. And I didn't mind being up there where the world had paused and nobody could see me or hear me. Just a few minutes of pretending…

I imagined telling Mum what I really thought.

Now listen, Mother, I don't want to go to any stupid clubs. You see, I don't like them and I don't really have any friends at them because I'm not very good at anything and I'm not interested either. Now you want to dump me in a place where I don't know anyone and I'll have to do a whole load more things that I don't care about. And I know how much it upset you and reminded you of Dad, even though you didn't say… but I did actually want to fix those lights. And I really liked doing it.

I didn't mean to think that last bit. And I knew I'd never be brave enough to say any of those things.

I sat down in the old dust and sighed. That's when I noticed the tidy pile of cardboard boxes that I was sitting next to. I decided to open the top one.

Inside there was an old Mother's Day card with crushed tissue flowers on the front, a lined notebook with big uncertain handwriting and pages and pages of scratchy drawings of a house with five-legged animals in it. At the bottom of the box were clumpy clay models and strange mixed-up creatures made from cardboard, wires, feathers and buttons. An elephant-giraffe with a long neck and a trunk, a hippo-bird with two clawed legs, and other impossible animals. It's funny how you can't remember making these things, even though you must be the same person with the same hands.

I noticed then that the cardboard box had a sticker on it. It said *Nell – aged four*. All the boxes had stickers saying my name and my age! Year by year, everything I'd made had been stored in a pile, getting taller every year. I looked inside some more of them. All the other boxes had schoolbooks and reports in them. How come I didn't make things any more?

That's when I saw a brown leather case behind the boxes, lying alone in the shadows under the eaves, under forgotten dust. It was a bit bigger than my school backpack and quite heavy. I heard things shifting inside as I dragged it over by the handle. The leather was worn, the seams grazed, like skin protecting the tender things inside.

There was no sticker on it with my name, but I flicked the catches open anyway.

Inside was like an ancient tomb, full of flat pieces of metal with holes round the edges, narrow strips like silver bones, scattered among ornaments and precious objects. I rummaged through the pieces and found a musical box and sixteen miniature painted horses. I liked the way one fitted in my hand with my fingers under its metal belly and its neck against my thumb. Its galloping legs were frozen in time, its silent eyes wide open. And then I remembered what it was.

Once, all the pieces had made a mechanical carousel, almost as big as our coffee table, but taller. I was four when I last saw the brilliance of it, when I last saw the lights and spinning horses. I opened the lined notebook again, the one from when I was four. That's what the pictures were! Not strange creatures with five legs, but horses with long tails, and they weren't in a house, they were on a carousel. And then I remembered the buzzing in my skin and brain, the laugh alive in my tummy, as I had crouched and gazed at the swirling, whirling carousel.

I held the strings of tiny lights. I could see the filaments inside, as fine as baby hair. I arranged the horses in a circle. I poked the wires from the lights into a black battery cylinder. My hands remembered what to do. The lights burned, white and gold and pink. I turned the handle on the musical box, heard the rusty chimes speed up and come to life. All the fragments lay around me, all the pieces. But I thought the horses kicked; I thought they were spinning beside me, as if they were alive.

"Nell? Can't you find it?" Mum called. "Do you need me to come up and look?"

I scrambled to scoop all the pieces back up, to hide them away again.

"No! Don't come up!" I said quickly as I snapped the case shut. "I've found it."

Then I wondered what would be in a box called *Nell – aged eleven*. And I remembered why I didn't make things any more.

4.

I CARRIED BOTH CASES DOWN FROM THE LOFT, WITHOUT Mum knowing. I hid the secret brown leather one under my bed.

That night I lay waiting for the noises in the house to tell me Mum had stopped turning and was asleep. And I was remembering the carousel and who had made it all. My dad.

Mum said he had always been drawn to lights.

It was his business, making spectacular lighting displays for spectacular shows. Then seven years ago he ran away to somewhere called Las Vegas with someone – called Susie or something – to see the biggest lights of all. We never saw or heard from him again. Mum had said he was probably too dazzled to remember he had responsibilities. She said we had a new life to live and that now we were free of the pointless dreams of a man who had betrayed us.

Mum couldn't have known the carousel was in the loft. She would never have let anything of his remain behind. What he didn't take was put in bags and binned. There were no reminders of him. So why was the carousel still here?

And then suddenly I remembered the tin girl, who stood on top of the carousel with her arms out and her head back as if she was about to fly.

I remembered waiting for her to turn round, to look at me, as she spun past. Looking at the sky, looking at me.

I got up and crawled under the bed. Quietly I opened the case and turned the metal pieces so they didn't clatter together, so Mum didn't hear and wake. But it was too dark and I couldn't find the tin girl, couldn't feel her in there. Where was she?

I got back into bed with one of the horses. The metal warmed in my hand. I could feel the ribs of thick paint brushstrokes.

I turned the horse, felt the smooth curve of its neck, its hooves kicked up in a gallop as it no longer touched the earth. I thought I felt the sway of its mane against my fingertips.

I dreamed. Horses pounded in my heart. Lights brightened, circled, turning faster, spreading wider until I saw her in the middle. The tin girl was real!

As tall as me, her skin reflected the dazzle of the carousel. She lowered her arms and turned her face to me.

"Where am I?" she whispered.

5.

W<small>E LEFT THE CITY AND ALL THE THINGS THAT</small> were familiar to me. We drove towards my mum's sister who I couldn't remember, towards my two cousins who I'd never met. Mum hadn't told me until we got in the car that I was going to be staying with two babies as well. When you're on your way somewhere, it's too late, even if you want to argue.

"They're five and seven – they're not babies,"

Mum muttered. She seemed miles away.

"How come I've never met them before?"

"People are busy; it's hard to make time. Families are like that sometimes."

The polite lady on the satnav told Mum to take the first exit. We turned off into a narrow road, then into an even narrower one between some hills.

"What will I be doing?"

Mum glanced over.

"Nell, what's got into you this last couple of days? Something's bothering you, so why don't you just tell me."

I couldn't tell her what else I'd been wondering about, like why the carousel Dad made was still in the loft and all the things to do with that. I was too scared of what she'd say, what she'd think of me. A moment passed. There were potholes and bumps in the road.

"I feel sick," I said.

"Don't be silly. The two weeks will pass in no time."

Which was not what I meant, and anyway it was wrong. Two weeks takes two weeks. Which is ages.

"No, I mean I really feel sick."

Mum pulled over, searched her handbag and fished out a travel sickness sweet, a bottle of water and a paper bag – just in case.

I opened the window and leaned my head out. The air smelled cool and clean. I felt the tickle as Mum curved my hair round my ear, a warm patch growing across my shoulder where she laid her hand.

"It'll be hard for me too," she said, "being without you."

I watched her expression, but I couldn't tell. She kind of looked lost for a minute. Then she drove away, saying we'd be there soon.

Ruts jiggled us down a lane only just wider than the car. We passed mostly green and brown things: trees and hedges, empty fields and gates. The satnav showed we were off the map, the car on the screen floating in nowhere. The only thing that seemed the same was the sky, the same as it was in the city, high and out of reach.

We dipped further into the valley, round a corner past a place called Keldacombe Farm and then Mum parked by a stone wall.

There were two small children sitting on the wall chewing red liquorice laces. Gemma, the youngest, had fair hair; Alfie had dark hair and flushed cheeks, like me. They wore muddy wellies, jeans with holes in the knees and baggy, home-made jumpers. Before Mum got out, she reached across and held my hand. I noticed how warm her hand was, how it changed the temperature of mine.

"Hello, Aunty Cathy," my cousins said together as Mum stepped out of the car.

"You're Nell, aren't you?" said Gemma, holding the lace in her teeth. "Everyone calls me Gem."

"Cos Mum says she is one," said Alfie.

"Is Nell short for Nelly?" said Gem. "Like the elephant?"

"No," I said, thinking it wasn't a very nice thing to say.

Alfie elbowed her.

"What? I didn't mean she looks like an elephant, cos she doesn't," Gem said, swinging her legs and shrugging away from Alfie. "Is it short for Nellina, then? Or Nellanie?"

"It's not short for anything," I said. "I'm just Nell."

Gem jumped off the wall and said, "You're going to sleep in our room, Just Nell."

Which made my eyes open wide and my heart sink.

Gem said, "Come on. We've been waiting."

Her hand was warm and sticky as she pulled me through the gate.

We followed my cousins through another gate between chicken-wire fences, sheds and coops, past a blue greenhouse, along a crazy path towards Lemon Cottage and its open door. There were ducks and geese wandering around the wide garden. The lawn and pond were speckled with feathers.

"They're here!" Gem called.

The geese swayed and raised their heads, honking at us like we'd caused a traffic jam. Their beaks looked hard, their eyes sharp, like they knew something just by looking at me.

Aunt Liv came out of the door. She wiped her hands on a tea towel and flicked it over her shoulder. She didn't seem to mind the birds as she waded through them. Her flowery dress swished over her knees and across the top of her wellies as she hurried to meet us.

She tucked her short dark hair behind her ear. Mum hugged Aunt Liv as if she was in a hurry, gabbling on about how kind she was to have me at short notice.

"I tried everyone I could think of," Mum said. "You were our last resort."

Mum has a way of saying what she thinks without thinking what she's saying. Then she listed foods I didn't like (fish, Marmite and salad cream – embarrassing) and how she expected me to behave (polite, kind, helpful) and said I would be no trouble.

Aunt Liv smiled, put an arm round Mum and me.

"Come on in. Gem's made cakes."

6.

Most of their jumbled home was in the big kitchen. There was a long wooden table half laid for lunch, half covered in toys and papers. Cupboards with no doors spilled out books and crockery, all mixed together. Bunches of dried herbs hung from a clothes line and a basket of ironing and a pile of folded clothes were heaped on a crumpled sofa.

Mum dropped her big black handbag on the sofa

and all the other things tipped towards the dip it made. A duck waddled out from under the table and dashed outside, but nobody said anything. It wasn't like our house with its shiny surfaces and everything tidied away and organised.

We sat at the table. All the chairs were different. Mine wobbled on the stone floor and Mum brushed crumbs off hers before she sat down and hung her jacket over the back.

"This one's yours," said Gem, reaching across the table to me with a cupcake in her hand.

"Have a sandwich first," said Mum, holding out a plate of egg sandwiches before I could say anything. She always spoke like that, cutting corners. Mum told Aunt Liv about the important conference that she had to go to the week after and how hard she'd been working to help organise it. I watched the butter cream squelch up on Gem's cupcake and the cherry plop off. Gem clambered down, picked up the cherry from the floor and stared at the ball of dust stuck to it. She looked at me, at the cake. Head down, she ran towards her mum and buried her face in Aunt Liv's dress, holding the cake up high so she didn't ruin it any more.

"Never mind," Aunt Liv said softly. "Nell's here for two weeks. Plenty of opportunity to make her more cakes."

"Yes, but I wanted her to have this one."

"I know, love," whispered Aunt Liv. "It was a special one."

The cupcake reminded me of the things I had found in the loft. Even when they're squashed or broken or bits are missing and they look a bit rubbish, they're still important. And right from that moment I thought my Aunt Liv was nice.

The kettle whistled from the old-fashioned iron

stove. Aunt Liv got up and steered Gem back to her own chair. She told us she was growing plants in her fields to make tea.

Mum said, "Tea?" Like that, like a question. "You can't grow tea in England."

But Aunt Liv told her they had their own microclimate in the valley and that things just needed the right conditions.

Aunt Liv and Mum were only alike in their faces and their skin. They both had a way of shaking their fringes away from their eyes when they looked up. But that was about it.

Mum chatted about her recruitment agency and everything else that was keeping us busy and therefore unable to visit relatives.

"And I need to get back soon, Liv," Mum said. "I'll fetch Nell's case from the car, then I ought to go."

She got up, rummaged in her bag to find the car keys. But I couldn't let her fetch my case!

"I'll get it," I said, snatching the keys from her hand.

I ran out, with everyone watching me dodge the flapping geese and ducks. I couldn't let her get that suitcase. I didn't want her to find what else I'd hidden in the boot.

7.

I RAN BACK TO THE CAR AND LIFTED THE BROWN leather case out of the boot.

I'd just wanted to see the carousel built again. That's all. And I wanted to build it myself this time. I'd hidden it in the boot when Mum wasn't looking. She wouldn't know and then it would only matter to me. Only I hadn't thought about how to get it into Aunt Liv's house without anyone seeing. I couldn't think how to do it without getting found out and I was about to put it back in the boot, cover it with the picnic blanket and forget the whole stupid idea, because now it was actually happening it wasn't easy or like I had imagined. And then I heard something. The thunder of thumping hooves.

I spun round. Galloping round the corner, pounding straight towards me, was a black-and-white horse, a dark rider hidden behind its flying mane. They hadn't seen me.

I dropped the case. All the metal pieces inside clanked as it slammed to the ground. The horse swung its side round towards me, skidding on the gravel. I leapt back to flatten myself against the car, but missed and fell. The horse screamed, reared up, its long mane billowing around it like a storm. I covered my head, curled up, held my breath.

And when you believe you're going to die because

the flying hooves are going to crush you, you can't help what you think. And what I thought in that moment was that I'd be dead and Mum was going to find the carousel next to me and then I wouldn't be able to explain and she wouldn't understand. She'd think I'd been hiding it all along. She'd be unhappy forever thinking I had betrayed her too. And then the tin girl was there in my mind and she whooshed around and turned her back and I shouted, "No!" because I thought she was going to leave me and somehow it mattered more than anything.

Instead, there was a cry, a thud, as the rider hit the ground. The horse stamped down beside me, brushing my arm with the long feathery hair on its legs as it kicked away from me.

For a moment the startled horse stood over me, throwing its head, its skin quivering. I could see me in its wide dark eye, a tiny me lying there on the ground. It snorted, its nostrils flaring. Then it turned and galloped away, its white tail streaming behind it.

From the verge behind the car I heard the footsteps of the rider.

"Help," I said.

Nobody came. But from where I was lying I saw a pair of small feet in black pumps tiptoeing past the other side of the car. I saw a hand reach out to the brown leather case and drag it away.

"Hey!" I said.

But the feet were running, running away with the case and the carousel.

8.

Mum leapt up, scraping the chair against the floor, as I stumbled into the cottage dragging the grey suitcase behind me.

"What happened?" she said.

I held out my hand so she could see the graze and the blood and the dirt.

My throat ached from not crying, from holding in the things I wouldn't be able to say. Mum brushed me down, got some tissues and antiseptic cream from her bag.

"There was a horse—"

"A horse hurt you!" Mum said, which wasn't what I'd said at all. "What were you doing going in a field with horses? They're unpredictable, dangerous if you don't know what you're doing. You're far more sensible than that. Really, what has got into you, Nell?"

"I wasn't in a field," I said. "The horse came down the lane and nearly crashed into me."

"What sort of horse was it?" said Aunt Liv, taking the grey suitcase from me.

"Black and white," I said, "and very hairy."

"It might be one of Rita's horses," said Alfie.

"I don't think so," said Aunt Liv, looking puzzled. She turned to Mum. "There used to be about a hundred of those horses next door at Keldacombe

Farm, but they've been gone for quite a while now. They're due to be sold soon."

Gem gasped. "Is there a hundred now?" Then she said in a spooky kind of voice, "Like the story about the hundredth horse."

"What story?" said Aunt Liv.

"It's like… I think it's if there's a hundred horses then something special happens."

"There were only ninety-nine at Rita's, though," Alfie said.

"No, but I mean if there are then the hundredth horse is magic or something… but I can't remember exactly now."

"Gem," Aunt Liv interrupted, "where did you hear that nonsense?"

But Gem was looking at Alfie, who was making a face as if he was trying to make her be quiet.

"Somebody told me in the playground, ages ago," Gem sulked.

Aunt Liv shook her head. She turned to Mum.

"It's just some silly old wives' tale."

Gem mouthed, *No, it's not*, and folded her arms.

Aunt Liv rolled her eyes and turned back to Mum, who had her hands on her hips, waiting for a proper explanation.

"I'll have a chat to Rita at the farm," Aunt Liv said. "See if she knows anything about the horse. Really, it's nothing to worry about."

"I think there was a girl on the horse," I said, careful not to say anything about the carousel case. "But I didn't really see."

My cousins looked at each other, their eyes wide. Aunt Liv sighed, like you do when you've just worked something out and wish you hadn't.

"Oh," she said. "Perhaps that means Angel's back."

I noticed Gem nudge Alfie and he shushed and glared at her.

"And what's that supposed to mean?" said Mum.

"Oh, nothing," Aunt Liv said. "There was a girl who used to hang around the horses on Rita's farm. There was some trouble. I think she was caught stealing at the supermarket."

Mum had a look on her face now that said, *Did I really agree to this?*

"Anyway," Aunt Liv said, as if she wished she hadn't mentioned it, "I heard her family moved away some time ago now, so nothing to worry about."

There was a heavy silence as Mum put on her jacket and tugged her sleeves straight. *Oh, good,* I thought. *She's taking me home again.*

"Well, as long as you're sure you're OK, Nell, because I have to get back now. I need to finish preparing for the conference."

I held on to her. Because I wasn't OK and I had nothing I wanted to stay for. Not now the carousel had gone.

"Don't worry, Cathy," Aunt Liv said. "We'll take very good care of Nell."

Mum and Aunt Liv had a private chat outside the door before Mum kissed me about fourteen times and squeezed me in a hug. I linked my fingers round her waist so she couldn't pull away. But she did.

9.

"Have you two been playing with the cart?" Aunt Liv said, picking up the clothes on the bedroom floor. "I thought I left it behind the greenhouse, but it's not there."

"No, Mum," Alfie said.

"Not me," said Gem, wriggling into her pyjamas.

"Oh, well," Aunt Liv muttered. "Perhaps I put it somewhere else."

I looked around the room. The walls were half straight and half sloping in Alfie and Gem's bedroom, like we were in the roof. There was a small low window and a big colourful mess under the bunk beds. There was also a mattress made up into a bed on the floor. I could tell which bed was mine, even though Gem pointed and said, "This is mine, this is Alfie's and that's yours."

My cousins squabbled about where they were sleeping because they both wanted to be on the bottom bunk nearest to me. In the end Aunt Liv put a pillow at either end and said, "Just for tonight, then back in your own beds."

It's funny, but when you're little like them, anybody new is really interesting.

When Aunt Liv had gone, Alfie crawled under the covers and came up next to Gem. They lay on their fronts with their chins in their hands and stared at me.

"Have you got a horse?" said Alfie.

"No," I said.

"Have you got a pig?" said Gem.

"No," I said, realising this game could go on for a long time.

"Have you got a monkey?" Gem said.

So I said, "I haven't got any animals."

Gem made a sad face. They whispered to each other.

"We've got a pig," said Alfie. "Her name's Maggie."

"She's a kunekune pig and she's going to have some babies," said Gem.

"Any day now," said Alfie.

They were quiet for a bit, just staring at me.

I couldn't stop thinking about the carousel. I'd found something unexpected, something that made me feel brilliant inside. Now it was gone and it left my stomach churning. I shouldn't have taken it in the first place. Isn't that what Mum wanted, what we had both wanted, though? Everything of his to be gone.

I suddenly felt far away from home, far away from everything.

"Do you want your mum?" said Gem.

She was right. I wanted my bed, my room and my mum.

"Lights out," said Aunt Liv, coming back and flicking the light switch.

She knelt down, tucked the duvet tight around me, held my hand to look at the graze.

"I feel sick," I said. "I want to go home."

She kissed me softly on the cheek. Her hair smelled like summer.

"I know," she said. "It always feels like this when you're away from your mum and you don't know anybody and you're not sure what to expect. That's exactly how you're supposed to feel."

I liked that she made it all right to feel that way; it made my eyes follow her as she went out and closed the door. But soon it was unearthly quiet. So quiet you feel you have to fill the silence up with some words.

"Who's that girl your mum was talking about earlier? The one who used to live here," I said.

I heard the shuffle of the quilt on the bottom bunk.

In the dark Alfie whispered, "She's called Angel."

"So that means she must be," whispered Gem. "She stole ninety-nine horses."

I thought about when Gem asked if Nell was short for Nelly, like the elephant. And that Gemma was called Gem, like something precious. My name doesn't even mean anything. And it rhymes with hell and smell.

"It doesn't mean you're it just because of a name,"
I said.

"How do you know?" whispered Alfie.

"It's obvious," I whispered. "Angels don't steal.
Everyone knows that."

I could hear Alfie's, and Gem's wide-awake breath.

"If they had wings, they'd be an angel then," Gem
whispered. "They might hide them under their clothes."

I turned on my side, curled my knees up and closed
my eyes.

"Nobody's got wings," I said. "And anyway, nobody
could steal that many horses. Not even an angel."

"Nell," whispered Alfie. "If you do see her, don't
tell nobody."

"Why not?"

"She'll probably kill you."

10.

MAGGIE, THE PIG, DIDN'T HAVE A CURLY TAIL. IT was straight and she wagged it, just like a dog. She lived in a brick house with a tin roof in a fenced-off area of a big field.

Aunt Liv had a few fields. She said Lemon Cottage was a smallholding, not a farm. She had lots of ducks, three chickens and one pig, but all the rest of her land was for growing things. The geese belonged to

Rita at the farm next door. Aunt Liv was looking after them for now until Rita decided what to do with them, because she was going to be moving soon.

"Gem, Alfie, you can help clean out the pen," Aunt Liv said. "Nell..." She looked at my red skirt and white jumper. "Perhaps you could check the water trough, see if it's full."

The ground was soft and lumpy with sticky mud, and ruining my shoes. Maggie followed me over, waddling behind me with her barrel belly and rolled ears and wrinkled piggy eyes. She nudged my leg with her flat piggy nose.

"What's she doing, Aunt Liv?" I said.

"Don't worry, Nell, she's just wondering who you are."

Well, I wished she wouldn't. I wished she would stop following me.

"Nice Maggie piggy," I said, and held my hands

up because she probably couldn't understand English. "Wait there."

Maggie's ears twitched towards me. She seemed to be listening. But she nudged me again.

She turned her back and flicked her tail against my legs. I supposed she wanted me to pat her. But there I was again, doing something I didn't want to do. I saw Aunt Liv look over, so I thought I'd better do it. Maggie took a step away from me as I reached out. I felt my shoes sinking. I heard the sucking noise as I tried to free them, as Maggie moved away. Too late. I fell down in the mud.

Maggie squealed and trotted back to her shed.

"Maggie can be a bit naughty if she thinks you don't like her," Aunt Liv said, running over, holding her hand out to help me up.

A clever pig then.

I didn't want my mucky fingers to touch each

other, so I stood with my hands spread and my arms away from my clothes until Aunt Liv said to swill them in the trough. Then she wiped them on her apron and I didn't want to say anything about that. I stared at the dirt stuck in the lines of my hands, like somebody had drawn them with a dark brown pencil.

We cleaned and filled the food and water bowls for the geese and chickens, and after lunch Aunt Liv told us to go and play in the garden. I didn't mind my cousins too much, but I wasn't sure I wanted to dig a tunnel to China with them. So I asked Aunt Liv if I could stay with her.

She nodded to Gem and Alfie, told them to get digging if they wanted to reach China before teatime.

"I've got some weeding to do," Aunt Liv said. "You could help me, if you like."

I think she could tell I hadn't done any weeding before.

"Otherwise there's a fence to repair and some herbs to plant."

I was definitely staying in the house today. I pulled at my muddy clothes. Mum would have said to get changed, immediately, but Aunt Liv didn't seem to notice dirt.

"Can I phone Mum?" I said.

"You could, only I think she's going to be busy preparing for the conference right now. Wait until this evening, then you can have a proper chat."

She tilted her head and tucked her hair behind her ear.

"How about you take some things over to Rita at Keldacombe Farm? Rita's not been herself since Mr Hemsworth passed away last year. She's felt rather down."

She pushed the hair away from my face and smiled. "But I'm sure a visitor would cheer her up."

My brain woke up. Rita might know something about the horse and also, even more importantly, the girl who stole the carousel case!

"You mean go on my own?" I said.

Aunt Liv looked at me for a long time before she answered. It was the most normal thing for me to say, but obviously not the most normal thing for her to hear.

"Of course. You'll be fine."

Aunt Liv gave me a box of eggs and a flask of tea. She explained how to get to the farm next door, which didn't really mean next door like at our house. You had to go down the track a bit, cut across a field and through a yard.

"Shall I ask Rita about that horse?"

"Good idea, Nell. And later we'll see about finding you some more suitable clothes."

11.

Keldacombe Farm looked like a giant quiet grave; the windows had that way of looking at you as though they dared you to find out what was behind the walls. Not creepy, sort of unknown. Like when you read someone's name on a gravestone and you know someone's under there, but also that they're not.

Nothing moved or made a sound except the

black rooks croaking as they swept away from the roof.

I walked towards the house. Grass and weeds grew through cracks in the yard between the stables, except near one door where the grass was flattened, as if somebody had walked over it.

The porch door was open. I thought I heard voices.

I know you're not supposed to listen to other people talking when they're in another room. I wasn't sure if I should go inside if Rita had someone else with her.

I called, "Hello?"

It went quiet for a moment. I stepped inside the hallway. There was a coat with dusty shoulders hanging there, two pairs of old boots. A grandfather clock looked down at me. Its silent ivory face had stopped at six o'clock.

"Anybody there?" I said.

A lady's voice. "Come on in, whoever you are."

Rita was sitting up against some pillows on top of a bed in her sitting room. Another house where everything seemed to have tumbled into one room. It was gloomy and smelled old, filled with dark wooden furniture and tarnished brass handles. There were packing cases along one wall, half filled with things wrapped in newspaper. The green velvet curtains were partly open, but the rest of the room was dim and I couldn't see anyone else there. I wondered who Rita had been talking to.

"My name's Nell," I said. "I'm staying at Lemon Cottage with my Aunt Liv. She asked me to bring you some things."

Rita didn't speak again straight away, but then said, "I don't get many visitors these days."

She had grey hair, with brownish-reddish waves grown out long ago.

"So you're Liv's niece. She mentioned you were coming to stay." She patted the bed next to her. "Sit, sit. Tell me all about yourself."

I sat on the end, but there was nothing to say. So I gave her the flask and said, "Would you like some tea? Aunt Liv made it for you."

A tired smile carved into her cheeks.

"How do you like it here?" she said, pouring greenish tea into a cup.

"I just got here yesterday," I said. "I don't know much about animals and plants and things."

She looked at my dirty clothes.

"It's not something you can read about in schoolbooks," she said. She gave me the cup, held her hands out, turned her palms over and back.

"See these hands?"

They were wide and freckled, with knotted knuckles, and they reached towards me.

"That's how you know, with your hands."

The cup was getting hot and I tried to give it back.

"Drink," she said. "It'll make your hair curl like mine."

She smiled, but I didn't get it.

"Take no notice. Just a saying. And Brussels sprouts won't put hairs on your chest either."

She laughed, but I still didn't know what she was on about.

"Go on, try it."

I tasted the tea and it was horrible. Like watery grass.

Rita chuckled again and took it away, then sipped from the same cup.

"Well, you can tell Liv I think it's delicious."

Then she put the cup down and knitted her fingers together.

"So what is it you wanted to tell me?"

Well, I didn't know what she meant by that either, but I was waiting for my chance to ask her about the horse.

"Aunt Liv said you used to have a hundred black-and-white horses," I said. "I saw one yesterday and my mum thinks it might be dangerous."

Before she could answer there was movement from the alcove in the far wall. Out of the shadows stepped a girl with long, dark, unbrushed hair, a big coat and a mean scowl. She stepped into the light and her eyes flashed sky-blue.

"*You're* the dangerous one," the girl hissed. "It's all your fault, jumping out and scaring her!"

"Now, now, Nell's just telling it like she saw it," Rita snapped. "Don't you mind her, Nell. Angel doesn't care much for people and being pleasant."

So this was Angel – the angel. And what I'd told Alfie was true: just because you're called something doesn't mean anything. This girl looked more like a mean pixie than an angel.

Rita reached for Angel's hand.

"Is it Belle we're talking about? What are you doing with her? She should be with the others at Old Chambers' farm; the auction is coming up soon."

Angel didn't take her piercing eyes off me.

"Old Chambers said I could look after her for a couple of weeks."

"Oh, he did, did he?"

"Yes, he did!" Angel shouted. "But now *she's* spooked her and Belle's got lost—"

Rita held on to Angel's arm, stopped her flying across the room at me, pulled her back.

"That horse knows this place even better than you. She won't have gone far."

Rita tried to look into Angel's face, but she wasn't having any of it. Angel shook Rita's hand away, came round the bed. I saw her feet. She was wearing black pumps.

"It was you!" I gasped.

But before I could say any more, Angel's eyes narrowed. She stared into me without speaking, right into me, mean and angry, as if she was trying to make me not say what she'd done. I backed away as she stalked towards me.

"Angel, now don't take on so," Rita snapped again.

But she wasn't listening.

"You tell anyone else you saw me," Angel whispered through her teeth as she ran past me, "and you'll never get it back."

12.

I DIDN'T DARE TELL ANYONE ABOUT ANGEL, NOT yet. Not now there was a chance of getting the carousel back. But why didn't she want me to say I'd seen her? I remembered Gem had said she'd stolen ninety-nine horses. Was it something to do with that? I hadn't even been in the countryside a whole day and already I'd decided I never, ever wanted to come again. But, while I was there, I was going to get that carousel back and I was going to build it.

Later, Aunt Liv took me into a charity shop in the village and made me try on things that smelled of washing powder and damp. She bought me someone else's jeans and T-shirts and jumpers, and a pair of blue wellies. It wasn't like fancy dress or anything, but I definitely didn't look like me any more. Or anyone I knew.

And then, just as we stepped out of the shop, some chickens almost flew into our faces. There were thousands of them! Scattered in the street and along the pavement. They ran into open shop doors, fluttered up on to walls and windowsills, *bok-bok-bokkahing* and flapping. People shooed them out of doorways and tried to collect them in their arms and herd them all together.

"Electric chickens!" shouted Gem. "You plug them in and out pops an egg."

"She means battery chickens," said Alfie, rolling his eyes.

"What?" said Gem. "You'd lay an egg if I plugged you in."

"And they're barn chickens, dopey," said Alfie.

"Liv, give us a hand!" someone shouted.

"Come on, children," she said. "Mrs Barker needs some help."

Soon loads of people had joined hands, trying to collect the escaped chickens into a big horseshoe shape between them.

"Nell!" called Gem, breaking the circle and holding her hand out. It was her face that made me join in, her happy eyes and tinkling laugh.

Nobody else seemed to find it funny and I don't think Gem was laughing because of the chickens. I think it was that giddy feeling of everyone swooping and tugging each other around.

We all shuffled together, towards the other end of the street, where chickens spilled in and out of a field.

A lady with grey curly hair wearing a checked coat and wellies was by the open gate, waving a long stick to guide the chickens back into the field. A collie dog lay pressed to the ground beside her.

There were long wooden barns down the end of her field and one of them was wide open. The chickens fluttered like bonfire sparks, ran into the open barn and back out again, as if they didn't know what to do.

Just then some of the chickens made a dash for the road again. One headed straight for me. It flapped into the air. And I caught it!

I could feel the spiny tubes in its wings and a warm bare patch of skin underneath, prickled with tiny new feathers. The chicken didn't wriggle, even though it made me run on the spot. Now I had it I didn't know what to do with it.

"In here." Mrs Barker pointed, reaching her stick around me to guide me into the field too.

Her dog thought she meant him.

"Down, Kip!" she shouted as he darted forward.

He dropped instantly, although you could see his shiny eyes desperate to scatter the chickens.

I crouched and held the chicken away from me as more chickens flapped past. I lowered its feet until they touched the ground. The chicken jerked its head and looked at a long piece of rope lying on the ground, tied to a metal pole.

"That's not a worm," I whispered.

It twitched its head and looked up. And I don't know why, but I couldn't let it go. Maybe it was because of its cross little eyes and the way its head was on one side, like it wanted to ask me a question.

I realised the chicken lived in a barn and maybe it didn't get to look out of the window very often. And then the tin girl was there, in my mind's eye, looking up. So I did too and I saw the sky was as blue as forever. And somehow I knew what that meant.

"That's sky," I said. "It's where you fly."

I opened my hands and the chicken ran back into the barn.

Mrs Barker closed the gate behind me, dragged her sleeve over her flustered face and thanked Aunt Liv for helping.

"This is my niece, Nell," Aunt Liv said. "She's visiting us for the first time."

Mrs Barker glanced at me, but was too agitated to smile back. She looked into the field.

"What happened?" Aunt Liv said.

"One of the barn doors was opened," she said. "And the main gate."

Mrs Barker closed her mouth tight, her face and neck red as the chickens' wobbly chins.

"I've been keeping Dorothy, my goat, in this field. And she's gone missing," she said, picking up the long rope from the grass. "If I hadn't heard she'd moved away, I'd know who to point the finger at."

"Who?" said Aunt Liv.

Mrs Barker looked at me.

"School holidays?"

I nodded. And then she said, "Well, keep your eyes open. If you should come across a girl called Angel Weston, you should steer well clear."

Which made my mouth clamp shut.

"Is it always like this here?" I asked on the way home.

Aunt Liv laughed. "What, you mean escaped chickens? No. But it's all rather strange. A horse and chickens on the loose and a missing goat."

77

"Maybe it's because of the fairy's tail?" said Gem, suddenly skipping along.

"She means fairy tale," said Alfie.

"That's what I said." Gem put on her spooky voice. "Maybe there are a hundred horses now and the hundredth one is magic and it's trying to set all the animals free."

"You can't even remember the story properly," Alfie huffed.

"Yes, I know, but it could be, couldn't it?"

Gem skipped over and clung to my arm.

"Do you think it is, Nell?"

"Are you talking about that hundredth horse story again? I don't even know it."

"Yes, but stories can be true." She was pleading now. "Can't they, Mum?"

Aunt Liv rolled her eyes and sighed.

"Well, stories are about us, about people really,

about what it's like to be us. But that doesn't mean everything about them is true."

"Maybe the hundredth horse is here and we don't even know it," Gem whispered, peering through the hedgerow as if there might be something hidden behind it.

I remembered looking in the box in the loft and finding the strange creatures I made and believed in when I was four.

"It's because you're only five, Gem," I said. "When you get older, you'll realise there's no such things."

13.

I PHONED MUM AND TOLD HER ABOUT THE ESCAPED chickens. She said, "You held a chicken!" and I said it was warm and soft and quite special. I told her what I said to it and she said, "I expect it listened to you," which made me feel nice. I said that I put it back, like I was asked, and she said, "I expect that chicken is looking out of the window right now, wondering about the girl who showed it the sky."

I listened to her soft breathing for a minute. I knew she was wondering the same thing too.

Afterwards me, Gem and Alfie wiped up the tea things. Gem made up a new word. She said because a shepherd is someone who rounds up sheep, we must be chickherds. You couldn't tell her any different.

"We're going to build our own farm," she said.

"She means a toy one," said Alfie.

"And it's going to have pigs, chickens, some magic horses and angels and everything. Come and do some too, Nell," she said, holding my arms and bouncing up and down.

I knew how she felt. It was what my insides did when I thought about building the carousel. I didn't want to see Angel again, but I knew if I wanted the carousel back, I was going to have to find her. I asked Gem and Alfie if they knew where she lived.

"She doesn't live here any more," Alfie said. "Mum said her family moved away."

Gem whispered in Alfie's ear, then Alfie whispered in mine.

"Sometimes she used to sleep in a caravan, back behind the farm," he said.

"Sometimes?" I asked.

"Sometimes she disappeared," whispered Gem.

I rolled my eyes: when you're five and seven, you believe anything.

"Why are you whispering?" I said.

Gem bit her lip. "Cos she never liked people going to the caravan."

I asked Aunt Liv if I could go out for a while and she said yes. I waited for her to ask what I was going to be doing, but she didn't. Gem said, what about making our magic farm, and I said, maybe later. Then she pulled my arm to bend me down so she could talk into my ear. "Angel knows the fairy's tail about the hundredth horse," she whispered.

I found Angel's caravan hidden among trees in the corner of the field behind Rita's farmhouse. I heard leaves shuffling, twigs snap. A startled rabbit zigzagged across the field. I took a deep breath.

The door of the mossy caravan was open. There was a comfy old chair, an empty packet of cheesy puffs on the floor. Nothing else but closed cupboards and an unmade bed.

I went back down the steps.

"What are you doing here?" said a mean voice from above me.

I jumped. Angel was standing on top of the caravan, half hidden in the tree branches and shadows.

"You scared me."

She laughed. I thought she muttered, "Good," but I couldn't be sure. She moved back out of the light between the branches.

"My name's Nell—"

"I know who you are."

My skin prickled and I almost forgot why I was there.

"I want my case back," I said.

I heard a shuffle, but she was invisible among the shapeless shadows.

"What's so special about some old brown case?" she hissed.

It wasn't what I expected her to say.

"You can't just take things that belong to other people," I said, irritated now.

I heard a small thump and then she was striding towards me from out of the shadows behind the caravan. She didn't stop staring, even as she walked past, so close, like she wanted to burn her eyes into my face. She gritted her teeth and scowled.

"You don't know anything."

I was suddenly wondering how she got down from the roof of the caravan so quickly. I leaned away from her as she stood right in front of me.

"Just give it back," I said. "It's not yours."

She pushed the hair away from her scalding eyes stared and stared. Then she snatched a laugh, screwed her eyes up.

"It's not yours either, is it?"

Well, it wasn't exactly mine. Not exactly. But how could she know?

"I haven't told anyone I saw you," I said, stepping back from her, trying not to breathe like I'd been running. "So just let me have it back now. Please. It's really important to me."

And as I said it, I saw something in her sky-blue

eyes, something I recognised, something that told me how she knew the case wasn't mine. She was hiding something too, just like me.

"Go away," she breathed, and disappeared into the trees.

14.

Bedtime. I couldn't stop thinking about Angel. She whirled around my head. I tried to shake away the feeling – we weren't the same, even if I was right about her hiding something.

"Your mum phoned again," Aunt Liv said.

I asked her for every tiny detail of exactly what she said until it sounded just like Mum and I didn't completely miss her when Aunt Liv gave me the kiss she'd asked her to give me. I saw Gem watching from the bottom bunk, her eyes flicking between Aunt Liv and me, her tired mouth slightly open. Then she asked Aunt Liv to pretend she was my mum and to kiss Gem to see what it was like.

And that was quite funny, because Gem kept asking her to do it again and again until Aunt Liv pinched her nose and said enough now.

As she switched off the light, Aunt Liv said, "Did Rita say anything about that horse?"

I'd forgotten all about the horse that Angel had been riding the day she stole my case. But I didn't know what to say. I was worried if I started talking about it I would say I'd seen Angel and then she would never give the case back.

"She hadn't seen it," I said.

"Still a mystery, then, hey?" She smiled.

I nodded.

The light disappeared as she flicked the switch.

"Nell?" a small voice whispered. "Did you see our farm?"

I felt bad. When your head is full of other things, when you're worried because someone has scared you and you didn't even get your case back, then the mini magic farm on the kitchen table only looks like a mess.

"I'll look at it in the morning," I said.

A soft sigh.

"Did you see her?" Gem whispered. "Did she scare you?"

I pretended I was asleep.

"It's all right. She scares everyone, Nell."

The darkness fuzzed in my eyes. I couldn't forget the way Angel had looked at me earlier. I didn't think she was mad at me because of the horse or because I knew it was her who stole my case.

I thought she was mad just because I knew she was here. Maybe that was why she wouldn't give the case back. Because if she did, then she wouldn't be able to stop me telling. Who, though? Rita knew she was here, and Old Chambers must have known too because she'd asked him if she could look after the horse. Who wasn't supposed to know? I thought about what Mrs Barker had said about her. The mystery of Angel spun in my head like the tin girl.

I didn't know what woke me. Maybe it was the moonlight on my skin. It was silent, except for Gem's and Alfie's sleepy breath. I got up and went to the window to close the curtains. The trees and greenhouse and sheds were etched in grey and silver. So was Angel. She was sitting on the grass cross-legged, collecting goose feathers from the ground.

She put them together in a fan, stretched her arm out and skimmed the air. Then she stuffed them in her pockets and skipped away.

15.

I DECIDED I WAS GOING TO NEED SOME HELP WITH Angel.

I asked Aunt Liv if I could go to Keldacombe Farm to see Rita again. Aunt Liv seemed happy I wanted to go, and besides she had a whole row of planting to do.

"Come back when you're hungry," she said, smiling.

Alfie watched me go. Gem was sitting on the floor playing with her plastic animals. She had her back to me, her arms folded.

"I'll help you later," I said, but she didn't turn round.

I went to the farm, called out and after a few moments Rita told me to come in. She was lifting things up and putting them back and opening drawers.

"Have you seen my blue cardigan?" she said. "I had it on the other day."

I helped look for a minute, but in the end Rita sat down on the bed, patted for me to sit next to her and asked what I'd been up to.

"Nothing much," I said, sitting on the end of the bed. "Except helping Mrs Barker get some of her chickens back in the barn. We couldn't find her goat, though."

Rita frowned, but didn't say anything about it. Then she smiled and said, "Tell me about where you live."

So I told her I lived with Mum and then did a list of the clubs and all my after-school stuff.

"Oh," she said, as if I'd just described the most boring things in the world. Which I had.

Then she told me about when she was a girl and how she used to get up in the middle of the night to start her day by bringing the cows in for milking. She helped her parents on the farm, feeding the animals, protecting them from the wind, the rain and the snow. She used to drink warm milk with a ladle from a bucket before school. She said it like it was a good thing. It was a bit like hearing about history at school, but better, because her stories were alive with moving, breathing things.

Then Rita sighed, saying that since she'd decided

to sell the farm and all the animals had been moved elsewhere it wasn't the same. She missed hooves clumping across the yard, geese gathering under the kitchen window, the tumbling bales of baked straw in the barns. And how everything had changed since Mr Hemsworth had passed away.

"He was very tall," she said, looking up as if his head was right there, just below the beam in the ceiling. "A real giant, with a deep, deep gentle voice that the animals could feel rumble in the ground. Sometimes I think I still hear him, but it's just the wind on its way."

You could tell she missed him most of all, that he wasn't a make-believe giant.

She took a long breath through her nose, as if she had just come up into the air from deep below the water.

"What have you got to tell me today?"

It's funny how she asked that again.

I moved across to the other side of the bed, suddenly realising Angel might be lurking in the alcove. But there was just a sewing machine on a little table pushed in there.

"Is Angel your granddaughter?" I asked.

Rita's eyebrows popped up over the cup of tea she was drinking.

"No, but I've known her a long time. She was always around here, with the horses mostly, or pinching something from the kitchen." She rolled her eyes. "She stopped coming, a while ago now. I heard her family moved. I expect they're back visiting."

I tried something else.

"Is she coming here today?" I said.

Rita leaned back. She looked surprised I'd asked.

"Why do you want to know?" she said, her head to one side, really looking at me.

"I… I just want to talk to her," I said. "I think she might need a friend."

It just sort of came out like that. But Rita's eyebrows popped up again and then she abruptly chuckled.

"Maybe you do too," she said.

I felt my cheeks burning. It's funny, but when you see someone is like you, just a bit like you, it makes you want to know more. I supposed that was it right from the start, what intrigued me. I was hiding the carousel and I wanted to know what Angel was hiding too.

Rita looked at me for a while, one arm folded, a finger tapping her mouth, her eyebrows furrowed. She seemed to make up her mind about something and beckoned me closer.

"It's not an easy task finding Angel, not if she doesn't want to be found," she said. "Go up towards the village, across the fields at the back. There's a circle of oaks at the top of the hill – you can't miss them. You know what an oak tree is?"

Her eyes twinkled as she smiled to herself.

"You might have seen a picture in a book."

I frowned. We had oak trees in the city.

"Of course I know," I said, remembering a picture showing the leaves had wavy edges.

"The leaves are barely out, so just look for the circle, ten of them. There's a chance you'll find her there," she said. "And take a couple of apples and some crisps from the kitchen."

"What for?"

"For you and Angel," she said. "You might need to do a bit of bargaining."

She lay back against her cushions and smiled to the room.

"Oh, and watch out," she called as I left. "That girl can tell a tall tale."

16.

I TOOK THE PATH RITA HAD TOLD ME TO TAKE.

On the highest hill overlooking the valley I found the ring of oak trees, their complicated branches still mostly bare. You couldn't see the farm or Aunt Liv's house from up there because of the woods and the way the ground seemed to sink away into a green plughole. But beyond the valley you could see miles and miles of fields divided into random shapes by the hedges, dotted with grazing animals. And a whole sky full of blue.

Something inside me was shaky and skipping.

A twig hit my head and I looked up.

Angel was crouched high in the tree, pretending she hadn't seen me. I saw her eyes flick down to me and away.

I had crisps, apples and maybe some useful information. Mrs Barker had wondered if Angel was here and had been the one to let her chickens out and steal her goat. And I wondered if there was more to know about Belle the horse than she'd said.

"Mrs Barker still hasn't found her goat. Maybe it was stolen…" I said.

I was only guessing, but Angel looked startled long enough for me to think I had guessed right.

"What are you doing up there anyway?" I said.

She scowled again, shifted her back against the trunk and pulled her knees up.

"You might fall," I said.

She rolled her eyes and looked away.

"I've got an apple for you," I said, holding it up high so she could see it. I pulled the bag of cheesy puffs out of my pocket. "And these."

Her face changed so quickly. I could have been offering her a thousand pounds. But I'd already guessed she wanted me to know she was there, that she'd dropped the twig on me.

"You come up," she ordered.

I went round and round the tree looking for a ladder or some way to climb up. I reached to the lowest branch but I couldn't hold on or pull myself up.

"How?" I said.

Angel smirked and then she laughed out loud.

"Easy," she said, "you're just not very imaginative."

There was a gentle thump and she was crouched on the ground looking up at me. Her dark untidy hair was tangled around her face and dark eyelashes. She was still wearing the long coat, which obviously wasn't hers, over black leggings and a faded black top and the black pumps.

She snatched the bag out of my hand. Her fingernails were chewed and dirty. She sat on a fallen tree branch, so I knelt on the grass nearby and listened to her crunch through the crisps.

"I'm staying with my Aunt Liv, just over Easter," I said, trying to be friendly, trying to lead up to asking her where my case was. After all, I was sure now she would give it back because I hadn't told anyone about seeing her.

"So?" she muttered.

She peeled open the side of the packet and licked

the crumbs from the bottom. She screwed up the empty packet and put it in her pocket and held her hand out towards me. I started to feel that it wasn't actually bothering her that I knew she had something to do with Mrs Barker's chickens and the missing goat.

"Apple," she said, only flicking a screwed-up glance at me.

I thought, *The cheek of it, like I'm her servant or something.* I had tried to be nice, but I smacked the apple into her hand. She laughed, like she was glad I was getting annoyed.

And I couldn't help saying, because she looked so smug, "You like winding people up, don't you?"

She lay back on the branch. She found that even funnier.

"You're really rude, you know," I said, getting more irritated. "I can see why Mrs Barker and my cousins told me to stay away from you now."

She was almost crying, laughing so much she nearly fell off the branch.

"You didn't listen, though," she said, her jewel eyes sparkling.

I huffed as hard as I could and stood up.

"I wish I'd never bothered," I said, and walked away.

I could hear her, almost hysterical with laughter.

"Nell!" she suddenly called.

I turned to see her trying to hide a smirk.

"What?"

"There's a *huuuge* spider on you!"

I screamed and flapped, brushing at my clothes.

"Where?"

"On your arm," she giggled. "No, the other one."

She rolled off the branch, clutching at her middle.

"It's on your back now," she gasped, hardly able to breathe.

I suddenly realised she was making me look an idiot. My fists were clenched, my shoulders up, as I stared at Angel rolling around in the grass, tears streaming through her high-pitched laughter.

She looked at me at last, barely able to control my own breathing.

"There's no spider," I snapped.

She took a last bite out of the apple, not laughing any more, but still smirking. She threw the core away and walked towards me, stared right into my eyes.

"I expect people told you not to believe anything I said either."

I groaned through my teeth and marched off.

I heard her footsteps behind me. I turned and punched my hands on my hips, only to find her mirroring me, standing just like me, barely able to stop herself from laughing again. I was NOT like her. And I was NOT going to give her the satisfaction!

I stomped off down the hill.

"You don't even want me around, so why are you following me?" I said over my shoulder.

"I'm not," she said, giggling.

"Yes, you are. Stop following me!"

"I'm going this way anyway," she said, then muttered, "So easy to wind up."

That did it. I wheeled round.

"What's down here, then?" I snapped. "Something else to steal?"

Her eyes quivered. I thought she was going to deny it.

But she smiled, like something really pleased her, like I'd played into her hands. Then she froze, her eyes still piercing mine, as a horse's neigh echoed through the valley.

17.

ANGEL TOOK OFF, ALMOST FLYING DOWN THE hillside, her tiny feet barely touching the ground, her long coat streaming out behind her. Even after all she'd said, like a magnet I was stuck with her, because she had the carousel case.

She jumped down from the top of the gate as softly as a cat and sprinted towards Rita's farmyard. Eventually I managed to get down the hillside, only tripping once, and scrambled over the mossy gate.

There were voices coming from the yard. I peered round the corner to see Mrs Barker talking to Rita. They were by an old Land Rover with a horsebox on the back, the driver's door open, the engine still running. Kip, the collie dog, was leaning out of the other open window with his paws on the edge and his twitching nose in the air.

We heard Mrs Barker say, "I'm just doing Old Chambers a favour and looking for Belle. I heard her neighing as I was driving down the lane. I thought perhaps she'd found her way back here."

"Well, I'll be sure to let you know if I see her or your goat," Rita said.

"Kip!" Mrs Barker called. "What're you doing over there?"

Kip had jumped out of the window and was

slinking across the yard, ears flattened. He crept, belly to the ground, towards a stable door.

Angel crouched, yanked me down beside her and put her hand over my mouth. Her eyes blazed.

"Your case isn't in the stable. Do something for me and I promise I'll give it back."

She took her hand away and I realised then she wasn't holding me there, not with her hands anyway. My heart was bumping and not just because I'd been running. I was wide awake, alive; the tin girl was spinning in my head.

"Do what?" I said.

"Think of something. You mustn't let her go in the stable."

Just like that, the answer clunked in my head: I had worked it out. Angel was hiding Mrs Barker's stolen goat in the stable. I don't know what made me do what I did next. I didn't stop to think why. I just wanted the carousel.

"I saw your goat!" I shouted, running into the yard. "It's up the hill by the oaks. I saw it."

18.

M<small>RS</small> B<small>ARKER</small> <small>TIPPED HER HEAD TO TELL</small> K<small>IP</small> <small>TO</small> get back in the Land Rover and then she left to go and find her goat.

Rita beckoned me over. Her hands were rough but warm as she held my chin up.

"Up on the hill, you say," she said. "Is that right, Angel?"

Angel appeared from behind the wall. Rita looked

at her, but Angel stared at the ground.

I had lied, but I thought Rita would understand when I told her the truth as soon as Angel gave the case back. Which was going to be any minute now.

"Well, this is a first," Rita said. "Now come on inside and put the kettle on, love. Three cups."

Angel didn't come. She must have gone to get my case at last because I'd helped her just like she asked me to.

I got the tea things from the kitchen and took in what we needed on a tray. Rita was sitting on the side of her bed.

"Why did you say this is a first?" I said. "Did you mean people can't normally find Angel?"

Rita put her cup back on the saucer. She was looking at me in that way people do when they're wondering about you.

"I meant that when they do find her they don't usually stick around very long." Her eyebrows were up as if she'd said enough. I saw her point. But then Rita said, "She doesn't usually let them."

And that was the moment when something inside me changed. Everything stopped in my head, all the wondering about what Angel might have done. A stronger feeling swept over me, one that made my insides ache. I realised I knew what it meant when you don't let people stick around. You're scared that they don't really want to know you, that when they do they'll leave you anyway. So you make yourself not care about them first. Maybe Angel and I were more alike than I had imagined. It was as if Angel had walked right inside me and I knew something about her, and myself, something more fragile than broken eggshells. It was as if those fragments were in my hands and I could crush them.

I realised then that Angel had come in the house and was listening, half hiding behind the door.

I poured some tea for her.

"Three sugars," said Rita. "Same as Mr Hemsworth used to have."

I stirred the sugar and carried the rattling cup and saucer over to Angel, as if it was the eggshells. And I could tell by her face that she was just as surprised as I was at what Rita had said. It was like going off the edge of the map. Who knew where we were now?

Angel took the cup without saying thanks and left me standing there with the saucer. She didn't have my case.

"Now sit down, Angel," Rita said. "And tell me what's going on."

Angel didn't sit and she started to say, "Old Chambers said—" but Rita was having none of it.

"I don't want to hear that Old Chambers is letting

you look after Belle. According to Mrs Barker, Old Chambers says the horse has gone missing and she's helping him look for her."

Rita took a breath and her voice softened.

"You didn't ask him, did you?"

Angel curled up on the window seat and raked her hands through her hair, messing it up even more than it already was. And that seemed to be a message to Rita.

"All right, all right," she said gently.

Rita took a step towards Angel, but then seemed to change her mind. And I knew too that Angel wouldn't be able to let her near.

"Angel, love," Rita said. "You know I have no choice but to sell Belle at the auction. Where is she? Did you take Mrs Barker's goat?"

Angel buried her eyes in her hands, under her wild hair.

"I can't find Belle," she said. "Don't tell Mrs Barker I'm here. You know she doesn't like me."

Rita tapped her lip. Her puzzled eyes tightened. She stared and stared at Angel. Angel wouldn't budge. Whatever secrets she was hiding, she wasn't going to tell.

"Drink your tea," Rita said. "I expect you're hungry too."

She went out to the kitchen and left us there, giving Angel a knowing nod, as if she was giving her the opportunity to say something to me. It was silent except for Angel sucking her tea up with her breath. So I slurped too. It's not the sort of thing I would normally do, but somehow it seemed just right. I saw her dazzling eyes turn up.

I heard plates being put out in the kitchen, the rumble of the microwave.

And what I was thinking just then was that I did

116

care about the eggshells in my hands and I could choose what happened next.

Angel uncurled in the window seat, her fingers smoothing the corner of the green velvet curtains, shaking her hair away from her face as if she had been pretending how much she was bothered by what Rita had said. I knew I was in the corner of her eye. I guessed maybe it hadn't been an act. But I couldn't really be sure about anything to do with her.

Then she muttered, "Why are you still here?"

I ignored how that made me feel. The door between us had opened and I didn't want it to slam shut again.

"Because you've got something of mine," I said. "And because you want me here."

She only looked at me for half a second, then closed her eyes and shook her head. My turn to play her game.

"That's why you took my case, so I'd have to come and find you," I said, glad I was getting a reaction from her. "And I'm here for two weeks and I've got nothing better to do."

I watched her eyes darting about under a frown.

"I wish you'd just go away," she muttered.

"But you tell lies. And," I said, realising I was getting her riled, "I want to help. I could take the goat back to Mrs Barker, then she won't have to know you're here."

I didn't know I was going to say that, but right then I knew I meant it. Then the frown and scowl were gone and Angel smiled.

Rita was in the doorway, hands on hips, interested in this bit of our conversation. But it was just for Angel and me. I held my ground and waited. Rita nodded to herself and returned to the kitchen. Cutlery clattered.

Angel left her cup on the windowsill and wandered around the room, running her hand over things, not looking at me. She came up behind where I was sitting on a stool. I thought I'd started to work out what Angel was like. She was probably making faces at me behind my back. But before I could put my cup and saucer down to turn around, I felt Angel's fingers combing through my hair. She started plaiting, turning my hair gently.

"If you really want to help," Angel said, with a smirk in her voice, "you're going to have to help me catch the goat first."

I felt the tug at the back of my neck when she pulled the plait taut and tied it.

"I thought that's what was in the stable!" I said.

She laughed.

"You guessed wrong."

I felt the plait fall against my shoulder, heard the

soft patter of feet as she ran out, snatching a plate of food and crisps from Rita in the doorway as she went.

Rita snuffed a soft laugh. She seemed to know Angel well, but it felt like I had joined in a story in the middle of the book. And now I felt like an idiot again. I'd got it all wrong and she still hadn't given back what belonged to me.

Then I realised that, even if she wasn't hiding Mrs Barker's goat in the stable, she was hiding something in there. She'd lied again, but I'd guessed what it was: Belle, the black-and-white horse. But I had no idea why, or what was really going on.

19.

THAT EVENING MUM TELEPHONED AND TOLD ME she was tired and only had a few days left to prepare before the conference. I told her I was wide awake and she said it must be the fresh country air, and I said or maybe the big sky and I could tell she was smiling. Afterwards I asked Aunt Liv if I could go out again and she said yes, but not for long.

I couldn't stay away from Angel and not just because I didn't have the case back.

The caravan door was open. I could see Angel sitting across the armchair. She didn't say anything when I went in, and she didn't seem surprised either, as if she had been waiting for me. She moved her legs and I sat on the warm arm of the chair where they had been.

"You promised you would give my case back," I said.

Her eyes narrowed. It made me want to take up less space on the chair.

"Tell me why you want it first," she said.

I wanted to be able to tell someone about the carousel, about how I needed to put it back together again and find the tin girl. I didn't want to be a liar, not like her. It's so hard to hide things. I wanted to tell someone. Should I tell her?

The longer it took me to answer, the fiercer Angel's eyes pierced mine. I could see her mouth changing, not smirking any more but smiling. And I knew I wanted to tell her, I wanted to share more with her. Then we heard footsteps running towards the caravan.

"Don't let them in," Angel whispered, slipping to the floor.

I closed the door behind me and hurried down the steps towards the widening halo of a torch.

"Nell! Mum says you've got to come see," Alfie said. "Maggie's having her babies. Now!"

Maggie the pig was lying on her side in a thick bed of straw, grunting and panting. She'd already had two babies, mini pink and gold and black piglets wriggling in the straw.

"I'm glad they found you," Aunt Liv said. "I thought you might like to see this."

Well, I did. And I didn't.

I decided I felt happier staying at the head end and watched Aunt Liv as she rubbed with a towel each piglet that was born. Then she passed them to Alfie and Alfie passed them to Gem and Gem held them out to me. And I thought about holding them, but I was too scared I might do something wrong, so she laid them with Maggie, telling her what she had named each of them – Grunty and Bunty and Humpty, all of their names rhyming. Aunt Liv spoke to Maggie gently, each time she grunted, called her a good old girl.

We were there for ages. It was dark except for the torch that Alfie hung on a hook above us. It made a warm yellow circle around Maggie and her staggering piglets. And then I started to see that they were actually beautiful but tiny and helpless until they lay with their mother. And you could just watch them all together and everything got more and more beautiful, right there in the golden straw.

I sensed something before I realised what was happening. In Aunt Liv's anxious hands. The way she moved away from us, out of the light, turning her body to hide what she held.

"Oh, no," she said softly.

Maggie had suddenly gone quiet, panting hard.

"Alfie, you and Gem run up to the house and call the vet. Take the torch. Now, please," Aunt Liv urged. "Nell, would you take this from me?"

The straw rustled under my knees as I knelt down and Aunt Liv handed me a bundle.

"I'm sorry to do this to you, Nell, but I need to help Maggie out right now," Aunt Liv said, and turned away. "I think it's too late, but try rubbing it."

She felt around Maggie, talked quietly to her, saying, "Come on, there's a good girl. Don't give up now."

I couldn't move, terrified of the tiny weight in my hands, of the loose little body wrapped in the towel.

"Nell," Aunt Liv said. "Just try."

I rubbed, scared and trembling. The piglet rolled silently between my palms. There was a piece of straw stuck to its glistening skin. It shouldn't have been there, but I couldn't touch it and I couldn't make it go away.

Suddenly I felt someone kneeling beside me in the shadows. Her! She took the piglet and swung it head first towards the ground. I reached out, thinking she was hurting it when it was already dead. She put her hand out, pushed me away. She stepped back from me, laid the piglet along her leg and scooped her fingers in its mouth. Silently and quickly her hands moved. She swung it again, blew into its nose, turned it over and rubbed.

She wrapped the towel back round it, laid it on my lap and vanished into the dark.

Alfie and Gem ran back in. "Mr Thomas is coming," Alfie puffed. "He'll be here in a minute."

"Thank you, Alfie. But I think Maggie's going to be all right, aren't you, girl? Look, the next one's on its way."

Aunt Liv looked over her shoulder at me, shook her hair away from her face.

"Nell?"

She reached out to take the piglet back from me. I unwrapped the towel and held it out to her. The piglet quivered; tiny black eyes looked up.

"Look," I whispered. "It's alive."

"Oh, well done, Nell," Aunt Liv breathed.

Gem hugged me and kissed the piglet.

"It's the magic, Nell," she whispered. "It's the hundredth horse magic. It's here and it's making you magic too!"

My mouth opened, but I couldn't say what had happened. Angel had come and made a miracle and nobody saw it except me.

I suddenly had a strange feeling. Isn't that what real angels did? Watched over and protected us just at the time between life and death.

20.

Early morning I raced round to the farm to
see Angel. Maybe she really was an angel. Maybe we
don't even know what one is.

She was in the yard. And she had become
someone else to me now, now I'd seen what she'd
done. But she looked like she was going to run away
from me.

"Aunt Liv let me name the piglet," I said,

following her across the yard.

She went to a stable door and closed it without looking at me.

"I called it Gabriel, after the angel," I said. "Like you…?"

I saw her startled eyes. I saw her jaw go tight, her cheeks blush, as she turned away and tied some string round the latch to keep it shut.

"I'm just saying thanks," I said. "How did you do it?"

Angel looked at me for just a second and then walked away.

"Really, I want to know," I said.

She carried on as if she was heading for the lane. I was almost shouting now, watching her back, staring at the big coat that covered her. Was she hiding something under there too, like Gem had said? Maybe the feathers that she'd been collecting.

What did she want them for anyway? I shook my head to clear the wild ideas that sparkled in my mind like glitter in a snow globe. I wasn't used to feeling like this. I just wanted her to stay.

"I didn't tell anyone it was you that saved Gabriel!" I said, staying put outside the stable where the grass was flattened. "I think I know what's in the stable. If you tell me, I'll tell you about my case."

It was all I had to bargain with. She stopped and turned back. There was a curve in the corner of her mouth. I saw the sky in her eyes.

"Help me catch Mrs Barker's goat," she said.

21.

"Shhh!" she said, turning around and pulling me down into a crouch. She clamped a warm hand over my mouth.

I was just trying to tell her how sweet Gabriel was (later Aunt Liv told me it was a she piglet not a he, but it was too late to change her name), that when I put her back down with Maggie, I just wanted to pick her right back up again. And I could see Angel was getting fed up with me going on and on, but that she was also trying not to smile.

"I get it. You love her," she said, as if it happened every day of her life. "Now shush. What do you know about goats?"

"Nothing," I mumbled through her fingers, "so don't go making me look stupid or anything."

Angel bit her lip to hide her smile and took her hand away.

"At first I really thought you had the goat in the stable," I whispered.

She glanced, her eyes narrow, but she ignored what I'd just said.

"Goats can be stubborn and Dorothy won't like it if you make a loud noise. When I took her—"

"You did steal the goat!"

"Shhh," she said. "I never said I didn't."

At least she admitted it. She told me what had

happened the day the chickens escaped, just like that, even though I didn't ask. She said she was stealing the goat from Mrs Barker and somebody went past, so she hid it in one of the chicken barns. But then the goat got scared of all the chickens squawking and flapping so she opened the door and then had to run because somebody was coming. She didn't have time to close the barn door and gate behind her.

"The chickens wanted to see the sky anyway," she said.

My mouth hung open.

"I knew that too," I said, but she had already moved on.

"The goat keeps getting away. She was in the stable—" She smirked because my mouth fell open again and I breathed in sharply. "But not when you thought she was." I closed my mouth again. How was I supposed to know what was true? She continued.

"I have to let Dorothy out, but she goes off into your Aunt Liv's fields because she likes to eat the herbs and I have to keep finding her," she said, like it was just ordinary, everyday stuff to her. "So, if we move slowly and show her something even nicer to eat, she'll follow us." Her eyes flashed. "Try not to spook her as well."

Which wasn't fair, but anyway I said, "OK. Where is she?"

She pointed ahead of us. "Just there."

The goat's head was pushed through the bushes, her chin and beard going round and round as she chewed.

Angel had some pieces of carrot and apple in her pocket and held them out. Dorothy the goat pushed her saggy middle through the bush and appeared in front of us. She had plump udders hanging down, bony hips and dirty knobbly knees. Her golden eyes were very interested in what we had in our hands.

Angel coaxed her down the hillside, feeding her small pieces of the carrot like they were sweets. Then she let me lure her into the yard with apple chunks. It made me giggle, Dorothy's soft lips nibbling at my fingers.

"You can go now," Angel said, tying some rope round the goat's neck.

"But I said I'd take her back to Mrs Barker," I said.

"Not yet."

"Why are you keeping her?"

Angel's mouth twitched from side to side.

"For the milk," she said.

"Oh," I said, wrinkling my nose. "Have you got that thing where you can't drink cow's milk?"

She seemed to think for a whole minute.

"No, I haven't," she said, frowning. "Just go now."

I wished she wouldn't do that. Angel had a way of

making me feel part of her, then as if I was nothing to do with her at all. But then she said, "If you go away now, you can come with me and find the horse later."

"But…!"

I'd thought Angel was keeping Belle in the stable! Had I got it all wrong again, like I had been thinking the goat was in there?

Angel smiled, as if she knew what I had been thinking. She seemed pleased that she was still able to keep things hidden and I couldn't work them out. Then I realised she knew I would be scared of the horse and wouldn't want to go. It hurt thinking she was pushing me away again. But then she said gently, "I'll come and get you later and we'll find Belle, and you'll see she would never hurt you."

I went back to Aunt Liv's, helped her box up some

duck and goose eggs. Which was a good way to try to teach Alfie and Gem the six times table. Then we sprawled around the table and I watched Alfie making moss hedges for their toy farm and listened to Gem make up stories about her magic plastic animals. And then Mum phoned and I told her about Gabriel and she laughed and said I'm glad you've found some special things there.

Later I went down to see Maggie with Gem and Alfie. We counted her piglets, all ten of them. We hung over the gate and kicked our legs up and watched them wriggling and guzzling. I saw Gabriel, the tiny one that Angel had saved, pushing her way in. I picked her up and didn't want to let her go.

I waited all day, but Angel didn't come. And I still didn't have the carousel, which was starting to seem like another made-up thing that didn't really exist.

22.

I woke. Something tapped at the half-open window.

I got up and looked down. Angel was standing on the lawn.

"What are you doing?" I whispered.

"Come on," she whispered back, dropping the stones she had been throwing at the window. "We're going to find Belle."

"Now? You said later."

"It is later," she laughed.

It was dark, but the moon lightened the inky sky. The garden was full of shadows; nothing stirred, except something buzzing in my brain.

"I can't," I said.

"Why not?"

And I was thinking, *Don't you ever listen to what your mum says you have to do?*

"Because I'm not allowed and it's dark and people don't go out in the night. We're supposed to be sleeping and—"

"What are you scared of?" she hissed. "Nobody's going to see us."

She shrugged and walked away. But there was something alive inside me. I did want to go. I wanted to follow her. Maybe I wanted to be even more like her.

"Wait!" I whispered.

I threw my coat over my pyjamas, put on my wellies and ran out to join her. I'd never done anything like that before – gone out in the middle of the night, without even telling anybody.

Suddenly she was standing in front of me, her eyes vivid in the silver light from the moon, a smirk on her face.

"Maybe you're not as chicken as you look," she said.

I let it pass. I didn't feel like a coward and that's what mattered.

Angel danced through the damp grass and I followed the dark footsteps she left there. She jumped from stone to stone to cross the stream while I tried to keep up. We wove through the trees, through the secret, bluish-black night, and soon we were brushing the mist and I was stepping on her shadow.

Angel caught my hand as we came to a clearing, made me stay where I was. She seemed to have heard something, but I couldn't see anything there. She called, "Yeeyeye."

I remembered how I'd first seen the horse called Belle, just as she was now, galloping towards us.

Speed lifted her mane – her nostrils were wide, her ears turned forward. The thump of her hooves came closer. I could feel something tight in my chest. I held Angel's coat. There was nothing to hide behind except her. Angel didn't move. All the air gathered at the top of my lungs because I couldn't see how Belle could stop. But she did. Like magic, half a step in front of Angel.

Belle was white as the moon, black as the shadows. She tossed her head and white waves rippled down her neck as she looked over Angel's shoulder at me. I heard her breath, how she breathed us in.

"Just look at her," Angel said. "Don't think about anything, just look."

I saw Belle's narrow face, her velvet, curved mouth, the long hair that fell from the back of her knees and swept the ground around her hooves.

Angel leaned against Belle's shoulder. There was nothing between them. Like they knew each other so well. And I knew that it was all right. That I would be too.

Belle's pink nostrils spilled steam into the air as she lowered her head and blew on me.

"Why is she doing that?" I said.

Angel laughed quietly. "She wants to know you. She will when you touch her."

I watched Belle's belly roll into gentle breaths. I saw the shapes of black on her white skin, or was it shapes of white on her black skin? I traced them with my hands, trying to find where one colour ended and another began. Just one hair's difference. Belle turned to look where I touched her. I saw the mirror in her eyes reflecting Angel and me.

"Do you feel it?" Angel said.

I felt the opposite of when I'd first seen her. Now I wasn't scared of how big and strong Belle was. I was thrilled to have her next to me, standing over us both as if she would protect us. I ran my hand over her warm shoulder, and I felt as if all that strength could be in me too. Belle made me feel brave.

"Belle wasn't trying to hurt you," Angel said. "It wasn't her that made you scared."

I thought back to what had happened when I first saw Belle. I was scared before I saw her, before I dropped the case. Because I'd taken the case and hidden it from Mum. Because I'd done something I shouldn't have. Or maybe because I was scared of what was inside it.

"I've never seen a horse like this one," I said.

"Some people call them gypsy cobs and some people call them gypsy vanners. They're like a mixture of other horses, but nobody really knows. Travellers bred them a long time ago to be strong enough to pull their caravans and to be gentle with their children. Belle is from a special family of horses: Mr Hemsworth told me once."

I watched Belle shift to lean against one leg, watched her test where she moved her hoof so she didn't stand on Angel's foot. Angel moved slightly. Neither of them watched their own feet. It was magic. Just them shifting their feet so each could stand where they needed to.

Angel put her arms up and took hold of Belle's mane. She bounced and climbed on Belle's back. She held her hand out to me.

"Coming up?" she said.

"Don't we need a saddle and some reins?" I said, stalling, because I'd never been on a horse before.

Angel leaned over further.

"You ask so many questions," she sighed. "Sometimes you just have to find things out for yourself." She gripped my wrist. "Hold on," she said.

I held on to her. And she pulled me up.

23.

BELLE CARRIED US THROUGH THE TREES, HER steady walk rocking us as if we were babies held by our mother. She took us out into the fields. She followed a path along the top of the hillside, a path like the spine of a great big humped creature. The birds were asleep, like we should have been. I felt like we were walking through their dreams. I didn't know it would feel like that.

Safe. All three of us moving together like one whole creature.

Belle stopped at the top of the hill. We looked up at the chipped milky moon. We were in the sky with it.

"The moon's got a little bit missing," I said.

"That's just a shadow," Angel said. "The whole moon's there, even though it doesn't look that way. You have to use your imagination, see it differently."

And I thought of that moon. How the whole thing is always up there, every night.

"Sometimes I wake up in the night," Angel whispered, "and I just look at it so I remember that."

Bluish-black, the sky seemed closer as if it had come down to wrap itself round us. Our feet dangled in the air, the stars were in our hair, the milky moon was right there and I could have touched it if I wanted to. I raised my arms and I wanted to laugh or sing or shout, so I called out, "Look at me. I'm up here too!" which made Angel giggle.

Angel clicked her tongue and Belle moved on and we leaned back as she headed down the valley. I put my hands behind me. Belle's hips swayed as she shifted her weight to steady us on the steep hillside. I looked back at the moon. But no matter how hard I tried I couldn't see the part of the moon that was hidden. It made me want to know more.

The field levelled out. Belle was warm and the rocking made me feel sleepy. I yawned and the moon blurred.

I leaned my head on Angel's shoulder, still wondering, half dreaming, about her.

"Gem said you must be an angel because of your name. She thinks angels hide their wings under their clothes."

Angel laughed, but didn't say anything.

"Tell me a story," I said. "The one about the hundredth horse."

Angel was quiet for a moment.

"It's just a fairy tale," she said.

I remembered being small and tucked tightly in bed, Mum lying beside me with a new book, the crackle of the pages as she turned them. I remembered that sleepy feeling when all the invented creatures and magic in a story seemed as real as they do when you are dreaming.

"I don't mind," I said. "Tell me anyway."

Angel looked up at the moon.

"A long, long time ago," she began, "there were ninety-nine horses that were looked after by a big old angel who was stuck on earth because he had lost his wings."

She shrugged to move my head along her shoulder.

"Far away there was a little girl... no, a princess,

who was locked in a... in a castle with nobody to look after her because there was a big battle going on outside. Sometimes the queen came and let her out and gave her some food, but she was scared and lonely. One day the princess opened the window and heard horses far away and they sounded so beautiful that she wanted to go and see them.

"She was very small and it was a long way down from the castle window, but one night, when the battle was really bad, she climbed out of the window because she thought the horses were calling her and telling her to come to them. She ran through an enchanted forest and crossed a dangerous river and found the horses she had heard. One of the horses came and greeted her and took her into the herd. The girl... I mean the princess thought there was something magic about the horses because they seemed to understand her language and she understood them. That special horse looked after her."

"What colour were the horses?" I said.

"Mmm… black. No, black and white, like the gypsy cobs."

"Of course," I said, guessing she was probably changing the story and making it up how she wanted it to be.

"Anyway, the girl was only happy when she was with the horses and so, whenever she could, she climbed out of the window and went to see them. She learned how to ride them and she felt free when she galloped across the fields and hills, as if she was flying away from everything.

"One day the big old angel saw her, but she didn't know he was a big old angel yet. She tried to run away, but he caught her. She thought he would tell the people at the castle and they would be angry with her, but he didn't. He told her that he didn't know anyone who could talk to horses like she did. So he let her come to see the horses whenever she wanted and he didn't say much."

As she talked, my tired eyes saw the moonlight reflect on something pale in Angel's pocket.

"One day she climbed out of the window and found her special horse standing under the tree, with all the other horses gathered around. The big old angel was lying in the middle of them under the tree. She only found out he was an angel then because he said he had to leave soon to go and get his wings. So she sat with him and the big old angel asked her why she came to see the horses all the time. She told him about the castle and the battle. She told him the horses didn't make her feel like she was bad or lonely or afraid. When she was with them, the war and the castle just seemed like an imaginary story. They made her believe that feeling free and brave was true.

"The big old angel was sad because he said he wished he had done something about that and now it was too late."

Angel was quiet for a moment. I could feel sleep coming, her story both vivid and soft like a dream.

"Before he left, the big old angel said he wished for one more horse just for her. He told her that one day the hundredth horse would come, and it was coming just for the girl to make her safe."

We were back in the woods. Branches like fingers were black against the moon. Jagged shadows fell upon us.

"What happened?" I said.

"He left to get his wings and she never saw the big old angel again."

The pale thing in Angel's pocket seemed to move. I don't know why, but I reached out to touch it. Belle stopped walking. Angel stopped talking. We were at a gate.

Angel slipped down from Belle's back, held the gate open. Belle stayed where she was. Angel climbed on the second bar at the back of the gate, rested her chin on her hand.

"Aren't you coming?"

I thought she was talking to Belle and then I realised I had to do something to make Belle walk forward.

"What do I do?"

"Well, you could kick her. You could shout at her. You could throw some food over there and she might go and get it."

Angel laughed softly, but her eyes were dark.

"That's not what you do, though, is it?" I said, determined not to look clueless again.

I shuffled forward, sank into the curve of Belle's back behind her shoulders.

"What now?" I said.

"Look where you want to go. Squeeze your legs a bit. Just kind of want her to go where you want to go."

"She's not going to gallop off or anything?"

I knew as soon as I'd said it that I shouldn't have. Even in the pale light I saw the disappointment in Angel's eyes. I felt like I had betrayed everything she'd shown me, interrupted some magic. So I just did what she said before the spell could break.

I looked, I squeezed.

And I laughed and Angel laughed when Belle walked right over to the gate, straight into Angel's hands.

24.

"Move up," Angel said.

She climbed to the top of the gate, stretched her leg over and curved it round Belle's wide ribs.

Belle walked on, clipping down the middle of the lane. All of a sudden I felt wide awake, as bright and alive as the stars.

"Tell me the end of the story," I said.

Angel sighed away a deep breath and continued.

"The girl took all the other ninety-nine horses to a safe place while she waited for the hundredth horse to come just for her. But then one day, while she was locked in the castle, some guards came and broke down the door and took her away because they said it wasn't safe there any more with the battle getting worse. They put her in another castle far, far away and it made her wild to be away from the horses. But she was trapped and couldn't climb out of the other castle.

"Eventually, after a long, long time, when they thought she wasn't as wild any more, they took her to another castle and she realised she could escape from this one. She climbed out of the window and travelled for miles and miles and found the horses again. And she's been waiting for the hundredth horse ever since."

I put my hand in Angel's pocket. She was quiet again. She smoothed Belle's neck. And I waited.

"Do you think she'll ever find it?"

Angel's voice was barely a whisper. "Of course she will."

I didn't care that the story was made up, that it finished abruptly. I just liked that Angel had told it to me. Not many people tell you stories. And I sort of understood what it was like for the princess waiting for something just for her. It made me think of the carousel. It made me think that looking for the tin girl was just like waiting for the hundredth horse.

I heard Belle's hooves crunch on the stony track as she stopped near Aunt Liv's.

"You're good at telling stories," I said. "But when it's real life, you should tell the truth."

Angel turned round, the moon shining in her eyes. "Some stories are true," she said.

What if it is true? I thought as I took my hand out of Angel's pocket and looked down at the pale goose feather spinning in my fingers.

25.

Alfie, Gem and me went up to Keldacombe village. Aunt Liv gave us some pocket money to buy Easter cards and chocolate eggs for each other. On the sweet shop door I saw a notice. It said: *Keldacombe Spring Parade and Fair.*

"Do you want to be in the parade too?" said Gem. "Cos we can ask Mum to make you a costume."

"What do you have to do?" I said.

"Nothing much. You just walk up and down," said Alfie. "People clap when you go past and then everyone goes to the fair to eat toffee apples. It's next Friday."

"It's a celebration of springs," said Gem.

"She means spring," said Alfie. "And we've got a cart to decorate and Mum's going to put some lights on it. Except she can't find the cart just now."

"This year we're going as peas," said Gem.

"Peas?" I said.

"Yeah, peas," Alfie said, his cheeks glowing, "because Mum is going to grow lots of sweet peas this year. She's going to be making something from the flowers."

"What, like tea?" I said.

"No, silly," said Gem. "Soup."

"She means soap," said Alfie.

"No thanks," I said. "I hate school plays and

things like that, where you have to be onstage with everyone watching. I'll just come and watch you."

Aunt Liv said I could go to Rita's to write out my Easter cards.

I liked the way Rita smiled when I came in, made room on her bed so I could sit there. Mostly I was hoping Angel would be there, though.

I thought about telling Rita that Angel and I had gone out riding on Belle and we'd found her now, and all the stuff that had happened in the night. But it was our secret. It seemed to belong to us and nobody else.

Rita chatted about the sheep and geese and horses and other animals she used to have on the farm. I tried to cover up my yawning so she didn't think I was bored – because I wasn't. I was just tired from being awake most of the night. It was like having another bedtime story, though, and I fell asleep.

"All this fresh air tiring you out?" Rita chuckled when I woke. She had been sewing. Scraps of material and worms of thread were scattered on the floor near the alcove.

"I didn't mean to fall asleep."

Rita nodded towards me. "Somebody left something for you."

The brown leather case was right there, by the bed! And seeing it at that moment was a million times better than when I first found it.

Rita smiled and handed me a cup of brownish tea.

"Try some. I don't know what Liv is putting in that tea she grows, but I'm feeling a lot more like myself today."

Which was funny because who else can you feel like? The tea tasted sweet but like mud. It was strange on my tongue.

"Angel stole the case from me," I said.

I wasn't angry with Angel any more. And it made my heart laugh to think I would never have met her if she hadn't stolen it.

"She gave it back, though."

Rita seemed to like that I said that. You can tell when somebody is smiling right through to their heart because their eyes fill with sunlight. I think right then we were the same. Exactly the same inside. Surprised by the things Angel did.

"What's inside the case?" Rita said.

"A toy carousel, with lights and music and everything," I said. "Well, that's what it used to be, but I won't know until I put it back together again."

And that made me laugh, because somehow it was a completely new thing now.

"Maybe you're starting to feel a little more like

yourself too," she said. "I don't think I've seen you smile until now."

My cheeks warmed. Maybe she was right.

"You won't tell anyone about this case, though, except Angel?"

"Who else is there to tell?" She winked.

"Can I go in the stables?" I asked. "I need some room to put it together."

Rita glanced up from threading her sewing machine.

"Use the one at the bottom on the right. It's dry and clean in there," she said.

"Oh, and do you know where Angel is?"

She'd kept her part of the bargain by giving me back the carousel case – eventually – and now I thought I ought to keep mine and tell her about what was inside it.

"She might be out in the yard," Rita murmured,

squinting at the tiny eye of the needle. "She might not. You know how it is."

Just then a clock chimed. A brassy, familiar tune.

Rita swivelled round on her stool.

"Well, well," she said. "I haven't heard that for a while."

I followed her out into the hallway and saw the question in her eyes as we stared at the ivory face, at the second hand ticking away.

"Was it broken before?" I asked.

"It was Mr Hemsworth's clock. He used to wind it up every day after work."

She reached up and unhooked a small brass key hanging on a piece of string from one of the coat pegs. It definitely hadn't been there before, I would have remembered. There had been two pairs of boots and a coat hanging there, but no key.

Rita ran her hand across my shoulders and rested

her arm there as we gazed up at the face. I could tell she needed someone to hold on to for a minute.

"That's the key to wind it up," she said. "Mr Hemsworth used to carry it in his pocket."

Angel wasn't in the yard. All the stable doors were shut. As I passed the flattened grass, I wondered if Dorothy the goat and Belle were in there. I wondered if they minded being together, seeing as they weren't even the same animal. But there was only one thing I really wanted to do. I hurried to open the case in the last stable on the right.

I turned everything out, pushed back the straw and tipped all the pieces out on to the floor. I touched them all. I recognised lots of the shapes, where they went on the carousel, what they made. I thought about where to start, what had to be made first and what was made last. I remembered the tin girl again. I shook the case, burrowed in the corners, felt behind the lining. She wasn't there. And I looked again because I didn't want to believe that she wasn't. Because what was bothering me, what was making me put my hands on my head and close my eyes, was thinking that my dad had taken her. And that meant I'd never get her back.

26.

"I must be going mad," said Aunt Liv. "The cart was behind the greenhouse after all."

We all made Easter biscuits with yellow marshmallows stuck on top to make them look like Easter bonnets. Or fried eggs, if you asked me. Me, Alfie and Gem were going to take them and trays of duck eggs in the cart up to the village to sell, but I was hoping we could hurry up and sell everything so I could go back to Rita's, back to the carousel. We raced down the path and I could hear Aunt Liv calling me, saying Mum was on the phone. I called back to tell her I'd phone her later.

We parked the cart on the village green. Gem still had sticky hands, but passers-by bought the biscuits from her and Alfie anyway. I stayed behind the cart and gave out change.

Mrs Barker was one of our customers.

"It was you," she said as I gave her some change. "You're the one that told me you saw my goat up by the oaks."

I had forgotten all about the goat! I had lied to Mrs Barker because Angel had said that if I helped her she would give me my case. And then she hadn't let me take the goat back after.

I nodded to Mrs Barker and took my hand away quickly.

"I thought so. Dorothy wasn't up by the oaks; she was in my garden this morning, tied up where I left her. Did you find her and bring her back?"

I didn't want her to find out I'd lied and that made me say too much.

"Maybe she found her own way home," I said. "Animals do that, don't they? I mean she's not the only animal I've seen running around on the loose."

Mrs Barker's head twitched. I knew she could see right through me. A goat wouldn't be able to tie itself back up again! Which made me talk even more.

"She probably just got fed up and wanted to go home. I know what that's like, because I'm away from home. And sometimes I just want to go back and sometimes I don't. It depends."

And then I worked it out. Of course! Angel must have taken the goat back. And I was thinking I could just be quiet now, but Mrs Barker said, "Other animals on the loose? What other animals?"

What had I said? I was also talking about Belle. I suddenly remembered that Mrs Barker was also looking for Belle to take her back to Old Chambers' farm. And Angel didn't want Mrs Barker to know she was here!

"Was it a horse?" Mrs Barker said, which made me knock the jar of coins over. They were spilling on the grass.

"Where's the horse now?" she said, even though I hadn't said yes.

"Nell?" said Alfie. "What about that girl on the horse the other day? The one down our lane."

"A girl?" Mrs Barker said.

I sucked in a sharp breath and bent down to pick up the coins to try to think, but then my elbow nudged a tray of eggs and they were about to fall. Gem caught them. I saw Alfie blush when I stood up again.

"That's what Nell said," said Alfie, looking at the ground.

He thought he was helping me! They were all looking at me now. Gem clutched my hand. I tried to tell Alfie and Gem with my eyes not to say anything more.

"Which girl?" Mrs Barker said.

When nobody answered, Mrs Barker nodded, saying, "It's her, isn't it? Angel Weston. She's back."

"Mrs Barker," Gem said, pushing in front of me so Mrs Barker had to step back. All our eyes switched to Gem. "You know the other day when your chickens got out and you lost your goat? Well, it might not be Angel doing it."

"Pardon?" Mrs Barker said, taken aback.

"Because you know that old fairy's tail about the

hundredth horse? Well, it might be here and it might be setting the animals free instead."

Mrs Barker's brow was furrowed, her nostrils wide. My shoulders sagged. This wasn't helping either. But then I saw that Mrs Barker was distracted from asking any more about Angel. I squeezed Gem's hand.

"What nonsense!" Mrs Barker said. "That old tale is about one bad horse spoiling the whole herd," she said, huffing and walking away. Then she called over her shoulder, "And, if anyone is going to spoil things around here, it would be Angel Weston."

When we got back, I was desperate to tell Angel what Mrs Barker had said, mainly because I wanted her to know that I hadn't actually told her that Angel was here. I felt sick again, hoping I hadn't said too much.

I looked in the yard and went into the stable where

I'd left the carousel all over the floor. The metal pieces were like the bones of a helpless creature. I knew my hands wanted to put them back together. And I stopped thinking about everything else and sat down.

I ordered the pieces by size, collecting all the bits that looked similar into piles. I started to lay them out, like a skeleton of the whole thing. When I touched the metal pieces, I could tell where to begin with the drum-shaped base, the spinning part in the middle and the black battery cylinder on top. I could see how the silver strips connected all the side pieces together. I could feel how it should look. But there was a tiny part of me that didn't want to see the carousel without that one special piece missing from the top.

I heard shuffling coming from the stable next door. I crawled over and put my ear to the wall.

I heard something shift against the other side of the wooden panel. A snort, the purring breath of a horse.

I went outside and saw the string was hanging loose from the door. I opened the top half of the stable. Goosebumps fizzed up my arms and prickled my neck.

Belle was in there. So was Angel. She was asleep, leaning against the wooden panel. A dark grey foal lay next to her.

Did this mean there were a hundred horses?

27.

I WANTED TO TOUCH THE FOAL.

"Can I see him?" I said.

Angel's eyes startled me, how bright they were against the dark skin under her eyes. She didn't tell me to go away.

The foal raised its head, rocked on to its side, swivelled its ears towards me.

"His name's Lunar. Like the moon," she

barely whispered.

"Hello, Lunar," I said.

I thought my hand might sink right through his rabbit-soft coat. Lunar was the colour of the deepest storm, a white stripe down the middle of his face, white legs, a pale fuzzy mane. He was wearing a blue cardigan with the arms chopped off, wrapped round

him and buttoned along his back like a back-to-front waistcoat. Rita's missing cardigan!

"Is he Belle's foal?" I said.

Angel nodded.

"Was he just born?"

"No, last Saturday at Old Chambers' farm. But I brought him here that night."

Belle blew through her nose and nudged the foal. He staggered to his feet. I took a sharp breath. Something didn't look right. His front legs stuck out at funny angles. He looked like a giraffe does when they bend down to drink water.

"Sometimes they get born a bit wonky," Angel whispered, seeing me look shocked as Lunar staggered to his mum and suckled. "He's got to stay in the stable to help his legs straighten up."

Angel watched me, blinking slowly, but didn't say anything more.

I watched Lunar sway as he came to me, nuzzling at my clothes. I saw the dark glass of his eyes, the curve of his jaw, the peachy skin of his nostrils, the wrinkles in his soft lip speckled with whiskers. Longer feathery hair grew from the back of his awkward knees and round his hooves. I felt down his strange legs.

"Will he be all right?"

Angel didn't answer. She was asleep.

I ran into the farmhouse. I had to tell Rita. Angel's eyes had told me that it was all too much for her.

"Rita, there's a foal in your stable! He's wearing your cardigan. And Angel found Belle too."

Rita raised her eyebrows.

"A foal! My cardigan?" She seemed just as surprised.

"Belle's foal: he was born nearly a week ago and

he's got a problem with his legs. Angel's been looking after him in one of the stables."

Rita leaned heavily against the kitchen worktop and muttered, "Why didn't Old Chambers tell me she'd had a foal?"

She shook her head and sighed heavily, rubbed her forehead.

"Let me tell you something about Angel," Rita said.

She rested her hand on my shoulder, and I knew we were now somehow together in this story.

"Belle was the first horse we had, long before we took on the herd. Mr Hemsworth chose her; she's from a fine heritage. Angel's mother was helping out here then. Sometimes..." She shook her head but continued. "One night Angel's mother was putting Belle in her stable. It was the night Angel was born. Right there in the stable, with Belle watching over them. You know, I think that from the first moment Belle raised that child. Taught Angel everything she knows.

"I'll let Old Chambers know Belle is here. We'll keep quiet about how she got here, though." She looked puzzled. "But he should have told me about the foal."

"Gem told me Angel stole all your horses," I said.

"Village gossip and tales," she huffed. "After Mr Hemsworth passed away, I couldn't look after the horses by myself. Angel led them over to Old Chambers' farm; he's been keeping an eye on them for me. I hadn't seen Angel since then, until she turned up the other day."

She sighed again wearily.

"Angel was a bit of a tearaway and perhaps someone saw her taking the horses over to Old Chambers' farm. People believe what they want to believe, make up stories to explain what they don't know."

Now there seemed to be another Angel, one that I was still getting to know. Rita appeared lost in the past for a moment. Then she squeezed my hand.

"I didn't know about the foal. Angel didn't tell me either."

So Lunar had been Angel's secret in the stable all along.

"Angel did steal Mrs Barker's goat," I said. "But she's taken it back now."

Rita shrugged and waved her hand in the air. She took the eiderdown off her bed for me to take out to the stable and put over Angel. Then she stopped gathering it into a bundle and laughed suddenly.

"The foal would have needed milk until Angel found Belle!" Rita tapped the side of her nose. "A nanny goat can stand in as a kind of foster mother.

Up on a couple of bales of straw, she'd be about the right height. Goat's milk is rich and almost good enough for a foal; Angel would know that."

"Really?" I said. But I was laughing inside, because now I knew why she had stolen Dorothy!

Rita was more serious now.

"You know, Nell, I think Angel is just trying to hold on to Belle a little longer. I won't deny her these last couple of weeks with her, with them both, before they go to auction. Come next Saturday, we'll all have to move on."

Angel was a thief, but only because she had been stealing some time with the things she loved.

Rita sat down then, as if something was too heavy for her to stand any more. "What to do?" she muttered to herself.

I went back to the stable. I covered Angel as she slept in the straw with the beautiful foal, Belle watching over them. I left some cheesy puffs and a flask of warm milk. Belle watched me close the stable door. I kind of liked what I saw. The three of them, like a family.

Back at Aunt Liv's the grass looked green, much greener than before. There were no goose feathers anywhere.

28.

IT WAS LATER IN THE AFTERNOON BEFORE I COULD go back to the stables, after we'd all been shopping at the supermarket. Gem had made two string bracelets and tried to tie one round my wrist and one round hers with a longer piece between, like a pair of handcuffs. But her funny knots didn't work and it all fell apart, and she gritted her teeth and sat down on the floor and yelled that she was going to make it again.

I raced back to the stable, to the carousel. I heard movement in the next stable, but I knew who was there now.

As I worked, Angel slipped in quietly, crouched and watched. Before long she had her finger pressed on the tiny nuts so they wouldn't spin while I twisted the bolts into the holes. And I didn't have to ask; she watched my hands and worked out what to do.

I showed Angel where to put the wires. The stable glowed with warm light.

"What's it going to be?" she said.

"A carousel, you know, like a merry-go-round with horses."

She gazed at it all, as if it was as precious as Belle and her foal.

"It doesn't belong to you, though, does it?" she smirked. "Otherwise you wouldn't be hiding it."

And I was going to tell her all about it, like I'd promised. I was, but I didn't like the way she said that. Poking and teasing. I wasn't going to talk to her about it while she was being mean.

"Mrs Barker asked about you again," I said. "But I didn't say anything."

Angel leaned back against the bales of straw.

"Why are you hiding from her?" I said.

She sank her hands into the pockets of the coat that was way too big for her. She looked up from under her dark lashes.

"Why are you hiding that case?"

She could sting like a wasp. And I was frightened now. We were like each other.

"Don't you see?" I said, smacking my hands down. "It's really important and I do want to tell you, but it's really hard for me to talk about it and you're just making it even more difficult."

Angel went out of the stable, kicking the door open. She opened the next stable so Belle could wander the yard and eat the grass growing through the cracks. Lunar came out slowly behind her, lowering his head, bright eyes searching the new surroundings. He staggered and skittered and wobbled. Angel didn't look back at him, but just like I had, the foal followed her.

I had put some pieces of the carousel in the wrong place and had to take it apart again. I wasn't going to give up, but it suddenly seemed too complicated.

I stood up, took a big breath and punched my hands on my hips. "Angel!" I shouted. "I want you to help me make this. I can't do it by myself."

Instead, Lunar came in. He lowered his head to get a closer look. I watched him shudder and skitter and come back to look again. His ears twitched and turned. I crouched and he lowered his face close to mine. He was the most beautiful animal I'd ever seen, face to face like that.

"Lunar was going to be put down."

Angel was half hidden behind the door, watching the shock on my face. Lunar staggered from my arms, back to Belle, to suckle his mother's milk. Angel sat cross-legged, facing me, her head down, her hair falling over her face. She talked, much more than she had before. She told me that she had been hiding out at Old Chambers' farm and that she had seen Lunar being born. Just then Mrs Barker and Old Chambers had looked in over the stable door, so Angel hid behind some hay bales. They saw Lunar couldn't stand, they saw his wonky legs, they said he wasn't right. She heard Mrs Barker say that nobody would want Belle with a foal like Lunar at her heels.

"She told him she knew a breeder, somewhere abroad, who would pay a lot of money for Belle, but they wouldn't want her if they knew she'd had a foal with bad legs. Old Chambers had to make sure that Mrs Barker bought Belle at the auction, then she'd make it worth his while. She wasn't interested in helping Lunar. She didn't even go in and look at him properly. She told Old Chambers to have him put down."

Her eyes looked hollow and scared as she stared over at Lunar. I hated hearing it, I felt sick, but something else was bothering me too.

"Why were you hiding there?"

She kicked at the straw, but wouldn't look me in the eye or answer. She just wanted to tell me the rest of what had happened. It was nice that she talked to me easily, like we had known each other for a long time. But that feeling wouldn't go away. Was she still hiding something? Was she lying? I screwed up my eyes to try to see her differently.

"I took your Aunt Liv's cart. Lunar couldn't walk far because of his legs, so I laid him in the cart and pushed him over here so nothing would happen to him. I went back and got Belle. That's when I saw you with the case."

We looked at each other for a moment. I felt so guilty then for what had happened to Belle. I'd dropped the case and spooked her. It had been my fault that Lunar was without his mother. No wonder Angel had been so mad at me. I squirmed; even my skin felt uncomfortable.

"The foal's safe now," I said.

Her eyes locked with mine. But she wasn't going to say any more.

I went back to the carousel. I concentrated, overlapping the metal pieces so they fitted together correctly. I felt the carousel horses wanted to spin, wanted to move, wanted to live. The shape grew and held. My hands seemed to know what to do. Somebody would want Lunar if his legs were better. What could I do? And like magic the answer was there in my hands.

"Look," I whispered.

I held up the tall cylinder from the middle of the carousel.

"We could make Lunar something to go round his legs, to help them stay straight. Surely, if his legs get healed, then someone will want to keep him. Won't they?"

Angel seemed to be sinking. Right into her coat. She was breathing heavily, shaking her head. I had a horrible feeling I had got something wrong again.

29.

Mᴇ, Aʟꜰɪᴇ ᴀɴᴅ Gᴇᴍ ʜᴜɴᴛᴇᴅ ꜰᴏʀ ᴄʜᴏᴄᴏʟᴀᴛᴇ ᴇɢɢꜱ.
We looked for shiny foil under dense hedgerows, in
the nooks and crannies of the trees, in the crumbly
terracotta pots in the greenhouse. We gave each
other Easter cards and rabbit-shaped chocolates. I
raced around to Rita's while Alfie and Gem hid all
their painted eggs and played the game again.

Rita was at her sewing machine with Angel

hanging over her shoulder, hurrying her, until Rita said to leave her be. Rita had cut up her green velvet curtains to make some padding for the foal's legs.

I could tell by the way Angel turned her back and looked through Rita's boxes that she was still hiding something from me.

The sewing machine buzzed. It made the air in the room feel uneasy.

Angel led Belle to the porch door, brought Lunar inside the farmhouse. He shied, stumbled and snorted at everything until Angel put her hands on him and made him calm.

We strapped the padding round the tender skin on Lunar's legs. We worked together fixing some splints to help straighten them. Rita used some leather straps from an old bridle to hold it all together. I wondered if Lunar minded that he was wearing an old blue cardigan and green trousers. I wondered if he felt different, like I did, wearing someone else's clothes.

"Will it help, Rita?" I said.

She smiled. "I've seen this sort of thing with foals before. He'll grow out of it soon enough."

And the one thing I thought about just then, the one thing I didn't want to think about, was how Rita, Angel, the horses and me would all be gone from the farm by this time next week. I wasn't waiting for the two weeks to be over any more, I wished they'd stretch out forever. But I was scared of wanting something impossible.

I watched Lunar while his hooves stomped on the floorboards and echoed round us. Angel paced round the edge of the room and I knew she was looking at me. And I could feel something uncertain prickling the hairs on my skin. Somehow it was too much and I wanted to be there with them, but I didn't. I don't know why, but right then I needed to phone Mum.

"I have to go," I said.

Angel ran after me, caught my arm as I was about to leave. She held my arm tightly and I wondered then if she was just as scared as I was of our time together being over. She had a cardboard box stuffed with straw. In the middle was Rita's tea cosy.

"What is it?" I said.

Angel lifted the edge of the cosy. Underneath were six white eggs, but not for boiling. Their delicate shells were chipped and cracked, pink creatures wriggled inside them.

"The fox got their mother," Angel said. "Keep them warm. They'll be out of their shells soon." She didn't look at me. "I know you'll look after them."

Me, Alfie, Gem and Aunt Liv spent all afternoon gathered round the eggs as they rocked and cracked. Aunt Liv lit the stove and put the box in front. The damp, strange creatures struggled to get out of their shells. We watched them dry, their feathers puff and lighten. We listened to their quiet whistles. Gem made up a song and sang it to them. It was called the baby geese song and it was funny and because I laughed Gem hugged me and said, "You're like our big sister-cousin." And I liked that a lot.

We held the goslings between us and made safe places for them on our laps; their soft feet padded on our palms.

In the evening they followed us outside and mingled with the other geese in the yard. We collected them up and laid them in the nest of a different mother goose. But she wouldn't settle with them. In the end, Aunt Liv said to put them with her special broody hen. The hen gurgled and clucked and fussed. She took the goslings under her wings. She spread her feathers and wiggled to cover them and keep them safe and warm. Then Gem told me a story about geese and I phoned Mum and told her too.

I said, "When geese are emigrating—"

"Migrating."

"*Migrating*, and one gets sick, two more geese fly down to the ground and look after it."

And Mum said, "Is that true?"

And I said, "Yes. They look after it until it can fly again."

And then she was quiet and told me she loved me more than anything.

30.

Rita had a message for me. Angel said to meet her at the oaks. As if we'd done it a hundred times before.

She was there with Belle. She held my arm and helped me up behind her.

"Where are we going?" I said.

"To see my family."

Belle carried us down the other side of the

valley, along narrow lanes where the hedges burst with bright new leaves and bobbles of buds. Our legs swayed against Belle's sides.

I'd really thought we were going to see her family and the people she was staying with. But she hadn't meant that at all. A herd of black-and-white horses grazed by a river in wide, open fields. They were just like Belle. Some more black, some more white, with long manes and long hair round their legs like feathery cuffs. We were near Old Chambers' farm.

Angel slid off Belle's back, opened the gate and went in.

"Yeeyeye," she called.

I saw their heads rise, their curious eyes and ears turning to her. I saw the horses come, slowly at first. They gathered and moved. I felt fear trembling in me as their hooves quickened. They came to Belle as she whinnied. My skin shivered with the sound and the rumble of their hooves. They came and surrounded us. I held tight to Belle's mane.

"What are you scared of?" Angel said.

I looked into the sky, into Angel's eyes. I saw the vastness there, the same wide-open space, electric blue. I didn't know what I was scared of.

The horses came to Belle; they blew on me. Belle walked through the herd, taking me with her.

"Belle's their leader, they follow her," Angel said as the horses came to her too.

"When I speak to them, I don't talk and they don't talk. You can just trust them because they understand that."

She walked among them as if she was one of them; she touched them all. She passed the young horses and they didn't run or shy.

"People are mostly scared of themselves," Angel said. "They get scared of their own brilliance."

People didn't know Angel at all. But the horses did. They trusted her, even if she was a liar and a thief. They knew her in a different way.

"We have to get Belle back now," she said, climbing up. "We can't leave Lunar for long."

We moved out of the field. The horses followed us to the gate, watched us leave. Angel's huge family. Maybe because of what she showed me I wanted to tell Angel everything.

"I live with my mum. Just us two," I said.

Angel kept looking ahead, at where we were going.

"I don't see my dad. He used to travel a lot because he worked on shows doing the lighting," I continued, knowing she wouldn't be mean this time. "I think he was clever and imaginative, but then he went away and didn't come back.

"He made the carousel, but I don't want Mum to know I've got it. I don't know why he left it behind, why it was still there. It's the only thing I've got of his – well, most of it. There's a piece missing."

"How do you know it's missing?"

She turned round. She seemed to really want to know.

"Because I know it was there before," I said. "And I think he took it."

"Like the moon?"

"The moon?"

"You thought a bit of the moon was missing. But it's not."

Angel turned away and Belle gently clipped along the lane.

And I wondered then if I'd looked properly. Had

I looked in all the corners, under all the lining? Was it there and I just couldn't see it?

"Do you think I might be like him? Like my dad, I mean."

"Do you want to be?"

"He was…"

What was I supposed to say? He didn't care about us; he betrayed us and left us. That's why none of his things, none of him or the bits of me that were like him, were allowed in our house any more.

"No," I said.

Belle stopped walking. Angel turned round and smiled.

"Mostly you're like you. Sometimes you're not, though. Sometimes you pretend you're nobody, just in case you are like him."

Then I heard her breath catch the rattle and

rumble of a car coming towards us. I could see the top of a Land Rover with a horsebox attached coming down the lane. In a moment Angel slipped to the ground, vaulted a gate and ran.

31.

Mʀꜱ Bᴀʀᴋᴇʀ ꜱᴛᴏᴘᴘᴇᴅ ʜᴇʀ Lᴀɴᴅ Rᴏᴠᴇʀ ɪɴ the middle of the lane. She stared through the windscreen for a long while before she got out and came over.

Belle lifted her head away from Mrs Barker's hand as she tried to stroke her nose. Angel had told me not to do that, that horses like to come to you first and then you'll know whether they want you to touch them or not.

"Liv's niece, isn't it?" Mrs Barker said. "What are you doing with this horse?"

Before I could even think what I was saying, I said, "I found her."

I was turning into a liar like Angel! Mrs Barker hadn't seen Angel though and somehow that was the most important thing.

She was smiling now, her voice gentle.

"I'll take her back to Old Chambers' farm. That's where she's meant to be, ready for the auction on Saturday."

I couldn't think what to do. Mrs Barker held my arm as I slid off Belle's back. She slipped a halter over Belle's head, led her into the horsebox. She told me to get in the Land Rover, that she'd take me home afterwards.

*

Mrs Barker drove to Old Chambers' farm. She left me in the car and talked to a man with a mucky overall and he nodded towards the stable where she had put Belle. They argued, but I couldn't hear what they were saying. Mrs Barker glanced at me, then came over.

"Do you know where this horse's foal is? Is it at Rita's farm?"

Mrs Barker tapped her lip when I didn't answer.

"The horses are going to auction on Saturday." She hesitated. "Belle's foal didn't look too good when it was born, but I persuaded Old Chambers here to keep it and I'd take them both on when they come up in the auction. So you see, if you could tell me where the foal is, then I'll make sure he gets looked after and stays with his mother."

That's not what Angel had told me. But people said Angel was a liar, and I knew she was too. Was it true what she had told me, that Mrs Barker wanted the foal put down? I was so confused. Something was bothering my stomach and my head and all my insides. And I couldn't think which secrets I was supposed to be keeping, and then I remembered how Angel looked when I said if Lunar was healed then somebody would want him. I didn't know what it all meant. But then I remembered those eggshells in my hands.

I looked everywhere but at Mrs Barker. As if I could find an answer somewhere, anywhere, in the sky, in the trees.

"Can I say goodbye to Belle?" I said, stalling.

I got out of the Land Rover and went into the stable. Belle hung her head and pushed her nose into my shoulder. I ran my hand along her neck. Lunar needed his mother. What should I say? What should I do? I looked into the dark glass of Belle's eye and I saw me. Scruffy, my hair unbrushed, but I was still shining there in Belle's eye. I knew the most important thing was to protect Angel.

"Mrs Barker… I'm not saying anything."

32.

THE NEXT MORNING MRS BARKER TELEPHONED
Aunt Liv.

She told Aunt Liv that her goat had gone
missing, again, and she seemed to think it might
have something to do with me. I hated being blamed
for something I hadn't done. I hugged my elbows in,
feeling like I was shrivelling to nothing.

I guessed Angel must have stolen the goat again

because Lunar needed the milk now that Belle was back at Old Chambers' farm. It was too complicated inside me. I didn't want to tell on Angel. I had promised I wouldn't tell anyone else she was here. Because she asked me. And because I wanted to. But it was so hard not to tell.

Aunt Liv sat beside me on the sofa in the kitchen so I didn't have to look her in the eyes. The soft middle of the sofa tipped us together. She asked me if I had anything to do with the missing goat.

"What if it's really important and I can't tell you?" I said. "What if it's a matter of life and death?"

"Life and death?" she said, lowering her head so she could look at my face.

"What if," I said, "you trusted me?"

Aunt Liv was as startled as me that I asked that.

"I mean, if I promise you I'm doing something for

the right reason, and I promise by Saturday it will all get sorted out, would you?"

I found Angel in the stable with Lunar and the goat. She spun round as I went in.

"You let her take Belle! What about Lunar? What do you expect him to do without his mother?" Her lips trembled.

"What was I supposed to do?"

Angel gritted her teeth and glared. "You could have—"

"No, I couldn't! I couldn't do anything!" I yelled. "And I'm in trouble and I've made my Aunt Liv trust me and I don't really know why. But I didn't tell anyone you're here with Lunar and Dorothy. So you're going to have to trust me as well!"

Angel smiled. Not the sort of smirky smile she usually had. Her eyes were watery and sad. She slid down the wall and crouched in the straw. She knew I was right. For once.

I undid the braces on the foal's legs so he could lie down and sleep. Already his legs looked straighter. Dorothy nestled beside him, chewing the hay. I looked at Angel crouched beside them, her arms wrapped tightly round her knees, the shoulders on the big coat sloping halfway down her arms. It was somebody else's coat, someone much bigger than her. She'd probably stolen it anyway. And it didn't fit, just like nothing fitted for her.

Angel's eyes were vivid. She moved away from me, climbed on the straw bales and sat at the top. She could see what was coming.

"Tell me the truth about Lunar," I said. "Tell me why I can't tell anyone else you're here."

She picked at some loose cement between

the bricks, not looking at me, studying each bit as if it was important. Stalling. Thinking of another lie?

"If I tell you," she said, "then you have to do what I say."

"Like what?" I snapped.

"Forget it."

"Is it something else bad? Stealing or something like that?"

"I said forget it." Her voice was quiet and heavy.

And I don't know why but I said, "OK! Just tell me!"

Angel tied a piece of straw in knots. And I waited.

"What do you want me to do?" I said.

"Nothing," she said. "I just wanted to see if you would."

"I said I would!" I snapped. "And I will."

And I was startled because I meant it and I didn't

care about all her lying and games and what was hurting.

Angel slid off the bales and walked right up to me, just like she had before. Her shoulders leaned in until her nose almost touched mine. She burned me with her eyes.

"They're… all I've got."

"Who? Belle and Lunar? What do you mean they're all you've got? What about your family and the people you're visiting?"

She stayed frozen, breathing loudly through her nose, her eyes blazing, my question hanging in the air like ice. I knew I couldn't give up. If she saw me back down at all, I'd never find out.

Car tyres tumbled over the gravel in the lane, rumbled into the yard. The engine stopped. Two doors opened, closed.

"Mrs Hemsworth?" a voice called. "It's the police."

I saw the fear in Angel's eyes as she stared at me, and I knew they had come for her.

"Why are they here?" I whispered.

She tried to listen to what was going on out in the yard, to the distant voices.

"I ran away." Her tiny voice was empty and cold. "They put me in a foster home and I ran away."

I could hardly breathe. No matter what I had already thought, I wasn't expecting that. I put my hand over my mouth so I didn't cry out.

"If you tell anyone, they'll find me and take me back. I don't want to go back, not yet."

Angel was still looking at me, pleading. We both turned towards the foal. The glass in his eyes was dark, almost black. Angel wasn't asking me to lie for her again. Now she was asking me to look after Lunar.

My heart ached. I nodded. She turned her back and I could hear the tears in her voice.

"Ask your aunt to bring Rita's geese back."

Then she ran. Out of the stable door, through the yard. Heavy thuds stamped after her. A woman shouted, "That's her! Angel Weston, stop! Come back!"

I looked through the crack in the door, saw Angel running up the lane, springing over a gate as a policeman and policewoman chased after her. Leaving Rita on the porch, her face buried in her hands. Leaving me holding Lunar, who was trying to stumble after Angel.

33.

Rita and I lay side by side against the pillows on her bed. Angel was a runaway. She had no family, no mother who looked after her. I knew what it was like to have my dad leave and not come back, but what was it like to be taken away from your family? It seemed a hundred times worse. A million.

I missed my mum just then more than anything in the world.

"They'll take her back, won't they?" I said.

Rita squeezed my hand.

"I should have known why she'd come here." Her voice stirred the emptiness in the room. "That poor child."

Nobody had called Angel that – a poor child. It was only because we now both knew why she had been hiding that everything started to fall into place. No matter what she had done, it wasn't her fault that her mother didn't look after her. That's why she wanted to be with Belle. She needed someone. Who else did she have?

Rita walked over to the window seat. She wiped the back of her hand over the dust on the window, staring at the grey mark it left on her knuckles. I saw how she tried to wipe it away, how the dust stuck in the wrinkles. She sighed many times. I couldn't help thinking how Angel had also turned to Rita when she had nobody left.

"Angel wants me to look after Lunar," I said.

I told her that Angel had said Mrs Barker wanted the foal put down, and that Mrs Barker had said the opposite. I told Rita I didn't know which story was true.

Rita closed her eyes.

"Maybe it would have been better…"

I knew what she meant to say. Maybe it would all be so much easier if the foal had been put down. My stomach tightened.

"How can you say that?" I said. "Lunar didn't do anything wrong. And he's getting better, you said so yourself."

"There's an old wives' tale," Rita said, "about the hundredth horse—"

"I know Lunar is your hundredth horse," I interrupted, "but it's just a stupid story. It doesn't mean anything!"

She held my eyes for a moment.

"Did Angel tell you that story?"

I nodded; my shoulders curled in.

"The one about the wild hundredth horse spoiling the herd?"

"No," I said, frowning. "Nothing like that. Angel told me a completely different story about a big old angel and the hundredth horse coming for the princess."

But all I could think about was what I had to do. Tears welled. I flopped in a chair and rubbed my eyes. I didn't know anything about foals or horses; I didn't want the responsibility of looking after Lunar. What if I got it wrong? What if I couldn't do it?

"I wish I'd never come here," I said, trying to stop the quake in my voice. "I wish I'd never met Angel."

Rita pulled up the stool and sat beside me.

"People think the worst of Angel. But there's another side to her not many people get to see.

"We had lambs one year," she carried on. "Three of them from the same mother, but she rejected them. They were tiny, too small and weak. They should have died by all accounts. Angel took them from Mr Hemsworth. He had a soft spot for that girl, not that he'd ever admit it. She was always at his heels, hanging around here. Angel nursed the lambs, kept them alive." She chuckled softly. "She dressed them in baby jumpers to keep them warm."

"Baby jumpers?"

Rita laughed. "Knitted woolly jumpers."

I supposed there were two sides to everyone. Sometimes people kept the bad things hidden. Angel seemed to keep what was good about her hidden.

"One thing Angel has never done is give up on

what she thinks is right," Rita said, more serious now.

I leaned against Rita, hid my face behind her arm.

"I thought I was just going to have a boring, ordinary holiday," I said, my voice muffled against her jumper.

"Perhaps you should leave this to me," Rita said. "I'll keep an eye on the foal. I'll get him back with Belle. Don't worry, I'll be sure to see they are sold together."

"Mrs Barker's going to buy them."

"She is?"

A question was bothering me too. When I said somebody would want Lunar if he was healed, why hadn't Angel seemed happy?

"Well, that's good news," Rita said. "Now you go on back to the cottage and enjoy the rest of your time here. Leave everything to me."

I could have gone. I knew that Rita would take

care of things, just like Mum had done when Dad left. But how could I leave knowing that Angel trusted me? None of this was Lunar's fault. And then what happened was I told Rita the truth.

"I'm scared, Rita, because I'm here without my mum and she always does everything for me. And she makes everything all right, but it means I don't have to do anything and I don't have to care about anyone. But I do care. I'm Angel's friend, and I've got a mum, but Angel and Lunar haven't."

I felt the warmth and the roughness of Rita's hand wrap round mine.

"When you really know someone, they get in here." She tapped at her heart. "Right inside." She looked at the wedding photo on the mantelpiece. "Then, when they're gone, you do what you can to protect yourself. You get angry, withdrawn, take it out on other people. But then what?" She smiled through watery eyes. "That shell you make round your heart, to protect yourself, stops others getting in."

She raised my chin.

"It seems to stop the goodness getting out too. Angel, you and me, we're not that different."

Her warm, strong arm pulled me to her.

"We know why Angel was hiding now. But what about you?"

As soon as she said it, I thought of the carousel. The one thing I had wanted to do was to put it back together again. I was good at doing the same things Dad did, but I hid the carousel because I didn't want Mum to know that I was like him, or to see me in the same way she thought of him. But was I also hiding another part of me? I thought of the tin girl about to fly and I remembered when Angel had said that people were mostly scared of their own brilliance.

Maybe that's the part I was hiding. And right then I knew I didn't have to be like him; I could be what I wanted. I would look after Lunar and I would never betray Angel.

"It's not Lunar's fault," I said, getting up. "What's he ever done?"

I fetched Rita's dusty coat and boots from the hallway.

"Come on," I said. "We're all he's got."

I went back to talk to Aunt Liv and told her Rita was looking after a foal and that I would need to be there a lot and asked if that was all right. Even though Alfie and Gem moaned and complained and Mum wanted me to call her, Aunt Liv still said yes.

"I won't ask any more because... because I know you have your reasons," she said. Her mouth twitched. "I don't know if you remember me talking about a girl who used to live around here, Angel Weston."

My stomach turned. If only she knew.

"I've got a funny feeling she might have something to do with all this."

Then I remembered what Angel had said when the police came. Even though she wasn't here, I wouldn't let her down.

"Can Rita have her geese back?" I asked.

Aunt Liv laughed softly. She didn't ask why. She touched my cheek and said, "I'll take them over tomorrow."

I went straight to bed, quickly falling into uncomfortable dreams. I heard the phone ring downstairs. I felt Gem kiss my cheek, smelled her sugary breath as she whispered, "Please can I see the foal. I love you."

I heard the shift of the covers as she and Alfie

climbed into bed without turning on the light. I heard the phone ring again. Then nothing.

34.

I WOKE EARLY AND RAN ROUND TO RITA'S, determined to do my best. Rita and me put the foal's leg braces on and walked him around. We took them off when he wanted to lie down. We made sure Dorothy had plenty to eat, and cleaned the water bucket and shovelled out the poop and made deep beds of straw.

I watched Lunar get stronger every hour. He

followed me. And that was the most wonderful thing. I didn't speak to him. He just decided by himself that he wanted to be with me. His soft muzzle nudged my hand or my back as if he wanted me to lead him, take him somewhere new. I took him in and out of the stables and around the house and to all the corners of the yard. He watched me build the roof of the carousel, as if he was waiting for it to come alive too.

"You're safe now," I told him.

And I wanted to tell him Angel was too. But was she?

Then Lunar's ears pricked when we both heard what sounded like a traffic jam coming our way.

I saw Rita's face glow as the geese swept into the yard, swaying and waddling and honking, Aunt Liv, Alfie and Gem herding them in. The geese huddled, shimmying away from the foal as he tried to chase them and play with them. They parted as he skittered into them, then they came together again and moved in the same direction.

"Nell said you wanted them back," said Aunt Liv.

Rita put her arm round me. "Did she now?"

She kissed my head.

"You know it wasn't my idea, don't you?" I whispered.

Rita nodded. She couldn't speak.

I wished Angel was there so she could see what she had made happen. I saw Rita shine as her geese came home; she laughed from her belly, as if the laughter came from very deep down. I did understand who Angel was. It was in the way Rita watched those geese, the way they brought her back to life. Maybe I was right all along. That is what real angels do. Bring things back to life.

I saw the trees uncurling their leaves, like

tight fists opening. I saw the sway of grass in the overgrown fields, felt the breeze against my skin, saw it ruffle the geese's feathers, puff under the foal's blue cardigan. It even felt like the cobbles under my feet were stirring. And I missed Angel because she wasn't there to share it with me.

"I love him," Gem breathed, her arms sinking into the mist of fur round Lunar's neck.

She knelt in front of him. He lowered his head and breathed on her. I saw her look into his eyes. I heard her whisper to him.

"I'm Gem," she said. "It means something precious."

She tilted her head to the side, nodding, pretending he had answered.

"I think Lunar is a lovely name too."

She nodded again.

"You are like the moon," she said. "And I love

you because you're the magic hundredth horse, aren't you?"

He nuzzled into her. She kissed his nose and rested her cheek there.

"Nobody believes you're magic. But I do."

Gem's sweetness made me feel happy inside. And I was thinking that there was no such thing as angels really. It was just people letting the goodness inside them out. And, when they do, everybody feels it.

And I thought about magic and fairy tales. They are not real. It's just that beautiful things make you feel full up inside. As if nothing is missing. And that feels like a miracle.

Rita had phoned suppliers and they had delivered some substitute milk for Lunar. He guzzled from the bottle, Alfie and Gem both holding on as he nudged and wrapped his tongue round the teat.

Dorothy jumped on to the bales and waited for him. When his bottle was finished, he went to Dorothy to drink some more.

Alfie's cheeks flushed. "Does he know that's a goat?"

"Course he does," said Gem. "Dorothy doesn't even look like a horse."

I heard Aunt Liv ask Rita if it was Mrs Barker's goat.

"Not a word, please, Liv," Rita said.

Aunt Liv raised the palms of her hands as if to say she wouldn't ask any more. She smiled at me and mouthed, "I trust you."

Gem couldn't take her hands away from the foal; when he moved, she followed. She kept talking to him, and in Gem's make-believe world, he answered.

Gem stared at the leg braces.

"He's just a bit wonky," I said, thinking she was about to ask. "They'll help make his legs straight. He's going to be fine."

"I know," she said. "He told me."

Alfie stood quietly next to Gem and said, "What else did he tell you?"

Gem looked uncomfortable for a moment, then she shrugged and said, "It's a secret."

Aunt Liv had also brought a big wicker basket hooked over her elbow, with a tea towel covering what was inside.

"I remember when the farm used to be like this," she said quietly, looking around at the bustling yard. "Thought you'd like to see these too."

She nudged a shy chicken out of her basket and into the yard, and the six yellow goslings that Angel had given me. The goslings formed a line and followed their new mother hen. They went straight into one of the stables. I wished Angel was there and I couldn't help thinking that this was where she would rather be. I ached inside, worrying about where she was now.

"Some kind of magnetic force is drawing the animals back to Keldacombe Farm," said Aunt Liv. She put her hand on Rita's arm and they held each other's eyes for a moment. "Are you sure you can leave all this behind?"

35.

WHILE LUNAR WAS SLEEPING, AUNT LIV, MY cousins and me walked up to the village. Tents were being raised on the village green, big lorries unloading, metal barriers being stacked to go along the street, strings of light bulbs going up between lamp-posts ready for the parade and fair on Friday evening. I saw a police car drive through the village, a policeman and policewoman scanning the streets.

They slowed and looked at us, then moved on.

We were there for a few things. I helped Alfie choose some green socks and Gem some green tights for their pea costumes for the parade.

When I got back to Rita's farm, the police car was parked in the yard. Rita was talking to the policewoman and policeman on her doorstep. I saw Rita nodding. They were still looking for Angel. My mind raced, as if I could find her just by thinking about her.

I stood by Rita's side and she told them Angel had been to the farm, but that we hadn't seen her since and we didn't know where she was. Rita said neither of us had known that she'd run away from the foster home. But the police didn't look convinced. They said we could both be in serious trouble if they found out we were hiding her.

They looked all around the farmhouse and in the

stables, but I knew as well as Rita that it wouldn't be easy finding her if she didn't want to be found.

While Lunar lay in the straw beside me, I carried on building the carousel. I fixed the struts across the roof, to make it stronger; strung the lights all around; pushed the horses on to their poles and into the roof. Everything was in its place, then the final metal disc went in the centre at the top. I flicked the switch. The lights came on, but the horses stayed frozen still in mid-air, mid-dance. Nothing moved. No spinning or whirling or turning.

Again I looked in the corners of the case, shook it, peeled back the leather, tore the lining away from the sides and reached in. I pushed all the spare pieces around, spread them over the floor. The tin girl wasn't there. And then I remembered why she was so important. She had a magnet in her. She had to be on the top! It wouldn't work without her.

I touched Lunar's soft, warm neck. I wanted to forget all the unfinished things, but I couldn't. Lunar slept, his breath soft as shadows, his blue cardigan and extra blankets keeping him warm.

"Where is she?" I said.

I picked up the spare pieces and threw them out of the stable. Angry at losing Angel, at the missing tin girl, at HIM for taking her.

Dorothy tottered out behind me. Her pale golden eyes stared up at me. "Go away," I whispered through my teeth.

Rita came across the yard. She saw what I'd done, but didn't say anything. She shooed Dorothy back into the stable with the foal and closed the door.

"The chicken and geese need putting to bed," she said softly. "Come on."

We held our arms wide. The geese were always

much quieter in the evening. They moved like water as we guided them into the stables. The chicken went up the plank to a higher shelf. The six growing goslings scrabbled after her. They ducked under her. Bits of their downy bodies poked out here and there. They peeped softly, jostling for a warm spot. The hen twitched her eyes and shimmied her feathers to tuck them all under her wings. The lines in Rita's face curved into a smile.

"Why are you leaving?" I said. "You like it here, don't you?"

She sighed.

"I was born and raised here. It's been my life. My parents left the farm to me and Mr Hemsworth. We had no children of course, but then we had our animals. But that's all gone now. I can't do it on my own."

I remembered Aunt Liv asking her how she

could leave all this behind and I knew we were both thinking about the people and the animals that were missing when Mrs Barker's Land Rover rattled into the yard. My heart rumbled with the sound of Belle as she whinnied from the horsebox.

"I asked her to bring Belle down," Rita said, standing up straight and pushing her shoulders back as if she was making herself stronger.

Rita invited Mrs Barker in and asked me to make a cup of tea. I listened to them talking as I hid behind the door in the hallway.

"Could be anyone bidding in that auction on Saturday and who knows where she'll end up," Mrs Barker said. "I'm prepared to pay for her now, before she goes to auction."

I heard the tea being poured.

"I've never known you to take an interest in horses before, Elizabeth. Your family have been rearing chickens for as long as I can remember. Why the sudden interest?"

"Look, Rita," Mrs Barker said, laughing a little, "I know Belle's from a good line and I'm prepared to pay more for her. I'll make sure she's well looked after. What do you say? Take the cheque and we'll say it's done."

A moment passed. "What about her foal?" Rita said.

I heard a cup being put down on the saucer.

"Old Chambers didn't think we should bother with the foal. But I'll make sure he's taken care of."

"So you don't believe in the hundredth horse myth?" Rita said.

"Bunkum," said Mrs Barker. "You don't believe it either."

"No, of course not. But I didn't know whether you did."

"This place is full of old wives' tales and other nonsense," Mrs Barker laughed. "Why would one more horse spoil the rest of the herd?"

Why were they talking about the hundredth horse as something bad again? That wasn't what Angel had said at all. The hundredth horse was supposed to be the one to come for the princess. I shook my head. BOTH of them were made-up stories anyway!

"Not before Saturday," I heard Rita say. "And I want Belle left here until then."

Mrs Barker didn't finish her tea. She led Belle from the horsebox, telling Rita she'd be back on Saturday morning before the auction.

Belle walked into the yard like she was queen of the place. She made the bricks and air and fields of the farm seem alive. She filled the yard with her call. But not until Mrs Barker left did Rita let Lunar come out of the stable.

We watched them for a minute and then I asked her, "Do you believe Mrs Barker, that she'll look after Lunar."

"I've no reason not to," Rita said. "Only I'd like you to tell me the story about the hundredth horse, the one that Angel told you."

"Why?" I said.

"I don't know," Rita said slowly. "I know it's only an old wives' tale, but the story everyone around here knows is to do with a wild horse and how that one wild horse turned the rest of the herd wild. You've heard the saying one bad apple spoils the barrel?"

I shook my head.

"It means that one bad person can affect everyone. And I'm beginning to wonder that if Angel told you a different story, then she might mean something else by it."

36.

ALFIE AND GEM PAINTED FLOWERS AND RAINBOW stripes on the cart to make it look nice. Aunt Liv went up in the loft and came down with a box of fairy lights and I used some battery packs from their camping lamps and wired it all to the cart.

"Are you going to look after the foal now?" Gem said as I left them with paint on their faces and hands.

I nodded.

"Good," she said. "He needs somebody like you."

And that made me go back and kiss her, and Alfie blushed when I hugged him too.

Rita was at her sewing machine. I took Lunar in to see her. She was helping Aunt Liv make Alfie and Gem's pea costumes for the Spring Parade.

"Would you like to see what I've got for you as well?" Rita said.

"For me?"

Rita beckoned me over.

"Angel asked me to make something for you."

"She did?"

Rita chuckled, but sadness reddened her eyes for a moment. Maybe she was thinking what I was thinking. I'd only be here for a few more days. We didn't know if we were going to see Angel ever again.

"Under the bed." Rita pointed.

There were frames made from coat hangers shaped into long, thin ovals. Rita had stretched white material over the frames, then sewn feathers on the top, just like real wings – made from black and white and grey goose feathers. The feathers that Angel had collected from Aunt Liv's lawn!

I held the wings and Lunar came straight over to look at them. He raised his head and snickered, his eyes wide and shining, but I didn't really understand what they were for.

I looked at Rita. All the words disappeared and neither of us could speak. Angel wasn't who people said she was. Rita and I knew that.

And then Belle whinnied from outside. We heard her hooves clatter on the porch and went out to see. We took Lunar back to her, but she was unsettled, lifting her head high, her nostrils breathing in big bellyfuls of air. She paced around the yard, Lunar pressed to her side.

"What is it, Belle?" Rita asked.

Belle called again, flicking her tail, tossing her mane. She looked to the sky, to the trees behind the farmhouse. I ran my hands over her, felt the stirring huge life in her, saw the black and the white of her skin.

I remembered the moon. I remembered how Angel had said that although part of the moon might be hidden in shadows, and you couldn't see it all, the whole of it was still there. You just had to use your imagination to see it differently. I looked around the yard. I didn't see what was missing. I saw what was actually there.

"Nothing's missing, Rita," I said, suddenly bursting with what I knew Angel had meant. "It's all still here!"

"What's all here?" Rita said.

"All the things that belong to the farm. They're all still here somewhere, even if you can't see them."

Rita chuckled. "You're starting to sound like someone else we know."

I grabbed her arms to make her face me, so sure I had to be heard, to try to make sense of what was whirling in my mind.

"Angel was right, Rita! Look!"

"I'm looking," she said.

"The chickens and the geese. Belle and the foal and the goat, and I know the goat's not yours, but that doesn't matter."

I had to wave my arms, because what was inside me was fighting to get out.

"And all your horses, Rita. They're not sold yet!"

I dragged her back into the hallway.

"The clock's ticking again, like a heart beating,

like it's alive, and it makes you think about Mr Hemsworth, as if he's here. That's what angels do, Rita! They bring things back to life. And she did it for you!"

Rita's hand held her mouth, her other arm tightly folded around her.

I thought of the carousel.

"Don't you see? It's like all the pieces of my carousel. They are just bits and pieces until they all come together. Then they make something extraordinary, something alive. Angel's been trying to put your farm back together again because it was so special to her too!"

The tin girl was there in my mind.

"Where am I?" she whispered.

I could hardly catch my breath, overwhelmed by what I suddenly knew. That one special piece that made everything else work.

"Angel's here, Rita! I know she is and Belle knows too!"

I ran. I knew exactly where she was.

The caravan was in shadow. The big coat was in a heap on the floor inside.

I went round the back and saw how Angel had been able to climb up and down. A plastic garden chair, a water butt on bricks, a piece of rope tied to a branch. I climbed up. It wasn't as easy as I thought it would be, but I could see why Angel had gone up there. From the top you could see if anyone was coming down the lane, or into the yard, or across the farm's empty fields. It was a good place for a lookout.

I looked up, stared and stared into the branches until my eyes were sure what they could see in the dark shadows and between the big hand-shaped leaves.

My scalp tingled. Angel was crouched on a branch high up in the tree.

"Come down," I said.

She didn't move for a moment.

"Nobody knows you're here. Just me and Rita."

It was harder going backwards to get down off the caravan roof. I didn't know how Angel had jumped down before. She still got to the ground before me.

I'd never seen her without the coat before. She was just a skinny girl, wearing the same scruffy clothes, who needed a bath and a hairbrush. She was just a girl that nobody looked after.

"Belle's here," I said. "Come and see."

We ran hand in hand back to the farmyard. I was just as fast as Angel until I let her go ahead. Belle didn't care what she looked like, or anything bad she might have done. Belle knew the inside of her, and so did I.

They lowered their heads. Angel leaned against Belle, as if there was nothing left of Angel. And Belle just stood steady, like an immovable mountain, with Lunar nuzzling at Angel's side.

I waited in the bathroom. Waited while Rita talked to Angel about how the police had been here. I sat on the floor of the bathroom against the bath and turned the taps on full, so they whistled with the pressure from the water. So I couldn't hear the things I didn't want to hear.

Rita opened the door, led Angel in and we left her to have a bath.

We sat in silence until Angel came out wearing Mr Hemsworth's bathrobe. It dragged on the floor behind her; it swamped her. That's when I knew the coat she'd been wearing was Mr Hemsworth's. A part of the farm as it used to be. She wore it so that Rita wasn't alone, so she wasn't alone either. She'd found the grandfather clock key in his pocket.

"Mr Hemsworth would have given the shirt off his back to see you were all right," Rita said. "I wonder what he'd be thinking now."

Angel chewed her top lip, but couldn't look at us.

Rita made a fire and we sat together, listening to the crackling wood. I brushed Angel's hair, untangled the knots. I plaited it. Rita made some sweet tea. What else could we have done for her?

"You know I have to tell the police you're here," Rita said.

I heard the hurt in her voice, that she didn't want to say what had to be said. I saw concern in her eyes.

Angel nodded.

I felt the panic in my stomach, in my throat. Why did this all have to be over? It felt unfinished, like the carousel without the tin girl. Like something was still missing.

"Not yet... please," I said. "Not until I go too."

Rita's mouth smiled and she nodded. Angel's eyes hung on to me just as I was trying to hang on to her.

"You look like you need a good meal inside you, girl. I'll make you something to eat."

Rita went out to the kitchen.

Angel went under the bed and brought out the wings that she'd asked Rita to make. She smoothed the goose feathers and then gave them to me.

"I don't understand," I said. "What are they for?"

We stared into the fire at the flickering life.

"You know when I came and helped with the piglet," Angel said. "And then the next day you asked me if I was an angel?"

I nodded. I remembered. I felt all the miracles she'd shown me since then.

"I thought that's why you were here," she said, "why you found me. I thought you might be an angel. Only you'd lost your wings so you'd forgotten you could fly."

37.

THE MOON WAS EXACTLY HALF MILKY WHITE, HALF hidden in the night when Angel and I arrived with Belle and Lunar for the Spring Parade.

That afternoon I had made some lights and wound them round Belle's halter. Angel and I had brushed her tail and washed the long feathery hair round her legs. We'd brushed her until she gleamed, the black shining, the white bright. We'd plaited her long mane and she looked beautiful.

Angel said Lunar had to keep wearing Rita's blue cardigan; she didn't want him getting cold. Rita had given us some coloured ribbons and we looped them through the edges and made bows and plaits and took off his leg braces. He seemed much taller than before and so proud of his straighter legs.

I wore black clothes, like a puppeteer on the stage, so I wouldn't show up against Belle and the foal and they would look as if they were walking on their own.

"You look like me," Angel said.

I scowled.

"Now I do," I said, trying not to laugh. But it was impossible because Angel giggled.

She messed up my hair some more and I practised smirking like her until she said to stop, her ribs hurt from laughing.

I had tried to tell her that someone would recognise her, but she wanted to come to the parade, to watch. She had no other clothes so I'd given her some of mine: my clean white jumper and red skirt. She looked like someone new too.

Angel put the wings on me that she'd asked Rita to make.

We stood in front of Rita's long mirror for a while, just looking at our reflections and wondering about ourselves and each other.

"Maybe we are two halves of one person," Angel said.

I realised then that I had been lonely for a long time. And I only knew that because I didn't feel like that any more. Because of Angel. Because we'd found the things about us that weren't different.

"Maybe inside we're exactly the same," I'd said.

And I knew because I felt like her that I would be

able to walk through the street with Belle and Lunar at the Spring Parade and not hide from everyone.

I smelled the air. Silvery metallic mist and dew, rich with toffee apples, hot dogs and onions. Light bulbs haloed. Music rang from the fair. We heard voices from the village murmuring, talking, laughing, waiting for the parade to begin. Angel hung back in the shadows as I went over to Aunt Liv, Rita and my cousins, who were waiting for me at the end of the village.

Alfie and Gem wore their green socks and tights and hats. They had paper flowers stuck all over their green padded round pea costumes.

"Ready?" said Aunt Liv.

My cousins each picked up a handle on their cart. Aunt Liv flicked the switch on the batteries. The flashing bulbs lit up the cart, the bamboo wigwams and their faces.

"All the way down to the end of the village, round the green and finish over by the fair," Aunt Liv said. "Rita and I will meet you there after."

We could see a stream of people dressed as morris dancers, scarecrows, milkmaids, pantomime characters, their faces bright with face paints going into the village; tractors rumbled and towed trailers with children in them, children dressed as witches and elves and other made-up things.

We were about to join the parade when I saw headlights splashing across the hedgerows as a car came up the lane behind us. Not the police, not yet!

I saw Angel about to run.

"Angel, love," Rita said, calling her, asking her to stop. "I know you want to be with Belle and Lunar, but I'll make sure Mrs Barker looks after them. I'll find a way for you to visit them."

"You don't understand," Angel said through her

teeth. "She's sending them away. They're going abroad."

Rita went to her, caught hold of her.

"You have to let them go, Angel."

Angel wriggled and slipped from Rita's hands. She struggled to speak, her wild eyes looking between Lunar and me. Belle's anxious hooves clattered against the road; her mane swayed wide as she tossed her head.

"Nell, I wasn't lying," Angel said. "He said the hundredth horse was coming for me. For me!"

We heard the car pull up nearby and the door open. I could see the blue of Angel's eyes, truer than summer sky. I didn't want her to leave, but I let her slip the rope from my hands.

She leapt on Belle and took off, Lunar at Belle's heels. But what did she mean the hundredth horse was coming for her? I remembered what Aunt Liv had said about stories being about us, about what it's like to be us. I stared at Rita, my mouth open. Suddenly it all made sense.

"The story, Rita!" I gasped. "The story about the hundredth horse is true!"

I didn't have time to explain. I ran as fast as I could, following Angel and Belle as they took off across the fields, Lunar behind them trying to keep up. The wind was in my ears, but I heard the car engine start up and I guessed the police would be coming around the lanes. I had to get to Angel first.

38.

I saw the open gate at Old Chambers' fields, but I couldn't see Angel or Lunar. Belle's head was raised high as she thundered across the field, the white of her skin etched in silver under the half-moon. She tossed her head and called the herd, the anxious sound prickling my scalp. I felt the rumble through the earth under my feet, I heard the thump of their hooves get louder, saw the flashes of white from their skins, as ninety-nine horses gathered and rushed from the far side of the fields.

I saw Angel with Lunar, Belle leading all the horses and galloping towards them. They pulled up and surrounded them.

I ran, calling to Angel. She didn't answer. I circled the wall of horses around her. But I wasn't afraid of the horses any more. I touched them and they moved aside and let me through.

Inside them all Belle stood facing me. She breathed me in. I touched her, she knew me, she trusted me. I could see half of the moon above us, half of it hidden in the deep night sky.

Angel was crouched beside Lunar. He walked over to me; his nostrils twitched as he breathed the air, his dark eyes shining.

"I know the whole truth now, Angel."

She reached up, her hands smoothing Lunar's shoulders. She shook her head.

"I do. The story you told me about the hundredth horse. You're the princess that…" I couldn't say she was the one nobody looked after. I realised how terrible that part of the story was for her. "You're the girl who climbed out of the window and rode the horses."

Angel trembled.

"There wasn't a big old angel, it was Mr Hemsworth, and they were his horses. You told him about what was happening to you and he wanted to help you, but he died and I'm sorry."

Angel folded her arms and buried her face.

"Mr Hemsworth wanted you to have Lunar because he knew the horses made you feel safe," I said. "He didn't have a chance to do it himself."

She looked up. The trembling made her watery eyes spill.

"He knew Belle was going to have a foal," she said, standing up. "But you're wrong about Mr Hemsworth. He must have been an angel."

She caught my hand, before I could speak, as she unbuttoned the blue cardigan and slipped it from Lunar's back. I saw the half-moon reflected in her eyes.

"You thought I was an angel. You kept wondering and staring at my coat, like I was hiding something under there, asking me about things, wondering if what Gem told you was true."

"You're not a real angel, I know that." I felt stupid again because she knew I'd been thinking ridiculous things.

"Not me," she whispered.

She put her hand over mine, put my hand where hers had been, at the top of the foal's shoulders, at the base of his mane. The hair pricked on the back of my neck, the blood drained from my face and I thought I was going to fall.

I lifted my hand and looked at what I had felt there: the folded stumps of bones, the softness of new feathers growing on Lunar's shoulders.

39.

I HEARD A CAR PULL UP AT THE GATE, DOORS opening and closing, lots of footsteps running across the field towards us. A voice called across the horses. It wasn't the police.

"Nell? Please come out."

"It's my mum, Angel!"

I went to go, but Angel caught my arm.

"Just let me speak to her. I'll come back."

"Will you?"

Two weeks away from home, from everything I used to know, and I suddenly remembered what life had been like. Waiting, hiding. Hiding myself.

"Nell, it's Mum. I'm here with Liv, Rita, Gem and Alfie." Her voice cracked. "Nell, please. I need to see you."

I helped Angel put the cardigan back on Lunar. My fingers trembled as I touched the feathers. I could barely believe what my eyes saw and what my hands felt. But I knew what I wanted now. I saw the tin girl in my mind. "I'm here," she said.

"I'm scared I won't come back too, Angel. And that I won't ever see you again."

"You'll go back to being nobody."

I felt the sting of her words.

"Don't say that," I said. "I'm your friend and I do care. I am somebody. You told me that. And you have to trust me."

It was there in the small curve of her mouth. How she told the truth, how it made me tell the truth.

"Don't tell them about Lunar," she whispered.

"Nell, please!" Mum called. "You're scaring me."

I had to ignore Mum, just this once.

"I didn't betray you before, Angel, and I won't now."

"Nell! If you won't come out, I'm coming in!" Mum called.

I heard the horses jostling, Mum still calling me, her anxious voice. Angel suddenly pushed through the horses. She made a path through them. She came face to face with my mum. Mum took a sharp breath.

"For a moment I thought... I thought you were my daughter."

I ran through the horses, hugged myself right into her.

"Aunt Liv called me at the conference and told me to come. She said I should be here. Are you all right?"

I looked at Mum. It was as though I'd never seen her before. Angel and I seemed to have swapped all sorts of things: our clothes and something inside. I looked at my mum as if I only knew the things about her that Angel knew about Belle. And nothing that had happened mattered, only what would happen next.

"This is Angel, Mum," I said. "We have to help her."

I didn't know why I'd said it. It suddenly all seemed impossible. What did I think we were going to do? Hide Angel and Lunar forever? Mum didn't know anything about Angel. She only knew about me. For her I was the same as when I last saw her.

"Tell her about the carousel," Angel whispered.

And it poured out of me like a tap turned on full, about the clubs and all the things that I didn't like. About finding the carousel. Why I wanted to build it again.

"I can't help some of me is like Dad."

Exhausted by everything that had happened, I had nothing left to hold it back.

"But I'm not like him. I won't do those horrible things he did to us. Will I, Angel?"

Angel shook her head.

"Mum, I'm nobody if I can't do the things my hands want to do. And I'm sorry I found the carousel Dad left behind and that I hid it from you, but—"

"He didn't." Mum's voice was flat and clear.

"He didn't what?"

"He didn't leave it behind."

The stillness then in the midst of a hundred horses was enormous, as I realised what she was saying before she said it.

"I kept it, Nell."

"But why?"

Mum turned her shoulder away. I needed to hear.

But she wouldn't speak.

"It's like the moon," Angel said. "Because you know something's there, even if you try to hide it."

Mum nodded to Angel.

"You know something about this?"

"She does, Mum. And so do I. I know you've done everything to protect us, to protect me. But Rita, she's the lady in the farm next to Aunt Liv—"

"I know who she is. I've spoken to Aunt Liv about what has been going on."

"You have?"

"You don't think I wouldn't want to know when I needed to be here for you? I've spoken to your Aunt Liv a hundred times these last two weeks and she's helped me realise that you needed to grow, you needed to work out things for yourself."

She wasn't angry. She wasn't deciding, telling me. Nothing.

"Rita told me that sometimes, when you keep the bad things hidden, you end up keeping the good things hidden too," I said.

Mum nodded. I wondered who she was. My mum. What we both thought about each other wasn't the same any more. In between school and clubs and everything else, Mum was always there. In the waiting and the driving, the bit in between everything. And in the middle of all those horses, we were someone else. We were... who we truly were.

"Do you know what I'm saying, Mum?"

"I do."

And then she said, "Hello. You must be Nell. What a mess, though." Mum laughed then. "No, it's not a mess, it's just something that needs organising. And that's what I do best."

Just then Lunar walked past us. His gangly legs trotted through the horses and we watched him go out of the circle of the herd to where Aunt Liv was standing with her arms round Alfie and Gem. He passed them, breathed them in and went to Rita. He nudged her back and made her walk forward. He pushed her until she walked through the horses. He brought her into the circle, over to Belle, over to Angel.

"I know, my lovely," Rita said, touching Belle. "You want your family back."

She reached her arms round Angel and Angel let her hold on tight.

"I have a question for you, Nell," Mum said. "You too, Angel. In fact all of you. What is it you want to happen now?"

Belle turned and stepped towards Mum. I looked in the dark glass of Belle's eyes. Saw my mother there. Belle blew on her and I knew why she wanted to know her. Mum was the one most like her.

I looked at Angel and we knew what we wanted

without speaking.

"To take the horses back to the farm," Angel said.

"We want to put everything back together again," I said.

Rita held Angel at arm's length and looked into her eyes.

"Bring them back," she said.

And, as we were about to do that, Gem ran over to Angel. She looked afraid for a moment and screwed her hands into little fists in front of her mouth.

"Hello," Angel said.

"Hello," Gem replied. "Lunar's the hundredth horse, isn't he? You told us a story in the playground and I remember it now."

Angel nodded.

"Lunar told me it was true," she said. "He told me he was coming to make you safe."

40.

Angel and me, we rode Belle with Lunar at her heels. We led a hundred horses back to Keldacombe Farm, thundering across the field, clattering along the lane, their breath spilling the mist around them. Mum drove everyone else back there in her car. We let the horses into the fields once more, saw the farm as it used to be.

Mum, Aunt Liv and Rita went inside the house.

The lights from the window without curtains glowed yellow in the dark yard.

Angel and I climbed on the gate to the field. We could hear the sigh of the horses' breath; we saw the white of their skins under the light of the moon, the dark of their skins hidden in the night. Lunar rippled among the other horses like a flash of magic. It was way past midnight. It was Saturday. The day of the auction. I would not sleep; I would not have missed a moment because that was all we had left.

Rita called from the yard. "Angel?"

And that's just what she looked like. An angel. Not because her hair was brushed and plaited or because she had my clothes on. But because we knew her. We knew everything she'd done was to keep the animals and the farm together. To watch over them like an angel would. It's what the horses and Mr Hemsworth had taught her. It's what Mr Hemsworth would have done if he could. Maybe Mr Hemsworth was an angel after all and maybe it was because of him that Lunar was who he was.

I saw the life in Rita as she came towards us, the life that Angel had brought back to her.

"Tell Rita about Lunar, about who he is," I whispered to Angel as Rita came closer. "Tell her what Mr Hemsworth said."

"I think there's a story you need to tell me," Rita said.

Angel took a deep breath and jumped over the gate. She fetched Lunar and he followed her back to Rita.

Angel held out her hand and took Rita's. I saw the blue cardigan slipping from Lunar's shoulders, I heard Rita gasp as Angel began to tell her the story of the hundredth horse.

*

I left them and went to the stable. I heard the music spring to life before I got there, the lights making a bright path to the open door.

The tin girl turned on the top of the carousel, looking at the sky, looking at me, her arms raised as if she knew she could fly. I thought I heard her laughing. I thought I heard her say, "Here I am."

And then I saw Mum sitting in the shadows, in the straw, leaning against the panels.

"You found the tin girl!" I said. "Where was she? I looked for her everywhere."

"She was with me all along," Mum whispered. "I've carried her around in my handbag for seven years."

SUMMER HOLIDAYS

TOMORROW THE SUMMER HOLIDAYS WILL START.
Mum and I are going to Keldacombe to stay with
Aunt Liv and Alfie and Gem. Rita said she wanted to
finish what Mr Hemsworth had never been able to –
to make Angel safe. She is Angel's foster mother now
and they live together at Keldacombe Farm with a
hundred horses.

Mum helped Rita organise some people to go and

work there and run the stables and a riding school.

Rita gave Lunar to Angel. She said that just in case the old wives' tale about the hundredth horse is true, just in case it spoils the rest of the herd, then Rita would keep her ninety-nine horses and Angel could have the hundredth horse. Which makes Lunar number one.

Angel had made up her own story about the hundredth horse, but all along the story was about her, only it was hidden inside the fairy tale. Rita said Lunar's story was in Angel's hands. They both believe that, because of who he is, he has to stay hidden. As he always was from the beginning.

But Angel and me both know that one day Lunar will want to kick, he will want to live and be what he is supposed to be.

Acknowledgments

Thank you to Jackie Morris, Artist and Writer, who introduced me to the beautiful gypsy cobs in Pembrokeshire, and much more. To Al Francis and Claire Butler who ran St David's Trekking Centre, which I am sad to say no longer exists. The inspiration came from you, and I wish you well. My thanks are eternal to family, friends and my agent, Julia Churchill, who continue to support me in every way. To Rachel Denwood who motivates me to work harder, Gary Blythe for the beautiful illustrations, and the team at HarperCollins who make it all work together.